(Continued from back cover)

Oh!
Could Christmas love
Be 'round the bend
For this lovelorn motley crew?
A blossoming happy family
Would make holiday dreams come true!

In less than two weeks he'd be gone…forever. There could be no happily-ever-after with this man.

And that was just fine with her.

Rachel waited until he shut the trunk, then she kissed him. Right out in the parking lot for anyone to see.

Surprise lit his eyes, even as a pleased smile lifted his lips. "What was that for?"

"Does there have to be a reason?"

"Absolutely not. But let's go home. With Mickie not there," Derek said, "it'll be a good time to get her gifts wrapped."

"If we have time. We might be too busy."

"What else would we be doing?"

"No child in the house. The two of us alone." She gazed at him through lowered lashes. "You do the math."

Dear Reader,

Sometimes the idea for a book's story line is so strong, the book practically writes itself. That was the case with *In Love with John Doe,* book two in the RX for Love miniseries. *The Christmas Proposition* took a little longer. When I first started writing it, I went in one direction then quickly realized I didn't like that path. So, I reined myself in, made some changes and let the characters take control. I have to say, I never envisioned matchmaking kids or that Mary Karen and Travis would be such strong secondary characters. So strong, that I'm hoping my next book out will be their story.

Anyway, back to this book. I'm really pleased with how it turned out. It was a lot of fun to write and I hope you enjoy reading it!

Warmest regards,

Cindy Kirk

THE CHRISTMAS PROPOSITION

CINDY KIRK

SPECIAL EDITION

Published by Silhouette Books

America's Publisher of Contemporary Romance

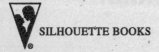

SILHOUETTE BOOKS

ISBN-13: 978-0-373-65570-0

Recycling programs
for this product may
not exist in your area.

THE CHRISTMAS PROPOSITION

Visit Silhouette Books at www.eHarlequin.com

Printed in U.S.A.

Books by Cindy Kirk

Silhouette Special Edition

Romancing the Nanny #1818
*Claiming the Rancher's Heart #1962
*Your Ranch or Mine? #1986
*Merry Christmas, Cowboy! #2009
†The Doctor's Baby #2040
†In Love with John Doe #2051
†The Christmas Proposition #2088

*Meet Me in Montana
†RX for Love

CINDY KIRK

has loved to read for as long as she can remember. In first grade she received an award for reading one hundred books. Growing up, summers were her favorite time of year. Nothing beat going to the library, then coming home and curling up in front of the window air conditioner with a good book. Often the novels she read would spur ideas, and she'd make up her own story (always with a happy ending). When she'd go to bed at night, instead of counting sheep, she'd make up more stories in her head. Since selling her first story to Harlequin Books in 1999, Cindy has been forced to juggle her love of reading with her passion for creating stories of her own…but she doesn't mind. Writing for the Silhouette Special Edition series is a dream come true. She only hopes you have as much fun reading her books as she has writing them!

Cindy invites you to visit her website at www.cindykirk.com.

To my editor, Patience Smith.
After all these years together,
I still think you're the best!

Chapter One

One of Derek Rossi's earliest memories was throwing a Wiffle ball to his dad. Since that day he'd pitched in more baseball games in his thirty-two years than he could count. Surprisingly, he'd never been hit. Until today.

He didn't even see the ball which dropped him to his knees. One minute he was talking with the coordinator of the Pitching and Catching Workshop, watching the boys and girls leave the Jackson Hole Indoor Sports Facility. The next, his head was pounding like a son of a gun. Derek blinked, trying to clear his suddenly blurred vision.

As if by magic a blond-haired blue-eyed angel appeared and knelt before him, her brows furrowed in concern. She smelled like vanilla and the bright lights in the gym gave her an ethereal glow. It didn't seem right to be on his knees before such a creature. He tried to stand, but she grabbed his arm and held on tight.

"Sit down." The warmth of her touch jolted him back to reality and told him this was no apparition. "I need to make sure you're okay before you start moving around."

The beating of the bass drum in his head nearly drowned out her words. Derek struggled to focus. "Are you a doctor?"

"Emergency room nurse." She held up her left hand. "How many fingers am I holding up?"

He squinted and the hand came into focus. "Two."

Her gaze met his and for a second he found himself floating, drowning in the azure depths... Until he became conscious of the noise—and the people—moving closer, encircling him, suffocating him.

The woman must have sensed his sudden distress because her voice rang out above the conversational din. "Everyone, back up."

"Come on, folks, move along," a man's voice echoed. "He'll be fine."

The crowd dispersed and Derek's panic subsided. Chatter turned to a distant hum. Ron Evans, one of the event's coordinators, stepped in Derek's field of vision. But the older man's focus was on the nurse. "Do you think we should call an ambulance?"

"No ambulance," Derek answered for her. The last thing he needed was more publicity. Besides, he felt okay. Or he would if his head would quit pounding.

"I don't think an ambulance is necessary, Ron. But an ice pack and some Tylenol would be helpful." The nurse's lips lifted in a rueful smile. "I'm afraid I locked up the first-aid kit a little too quickly."

"Coming right up," Ron said, hurrying off.

Even as she reached into her purse and pulled out a penlight, the nurse's attention didn't waver from Derek's face.

A light flashed in his left eye. He jerked back.

"Hold steady," she said in a voice that was soothing yet brooked no argument.

He did as she asked and the light flashed again.

"Your pupils react well to the light," she said in a professional tone he found reassuring. "How's your vision?"

"Fuzzy but getting better." He rubbed the spot just above his left temple. "My head sure hurts."

"Ron should be back any second." Even though the nurse's expression remained composed, her gaze lingered on his head, on the knot that he could feel growing larger by the second. "Can you tell me who you are?"

He may have only been in Jackson Hole a short time, but there'd been lots of buzz about the baseball workshop he was holding this first weekend in December.

"I'm Derek Rossi," he said, surprised she hadn't recognized him.

As if she'd read his mind, her lips quirked upward. "I know who you are. I just needed to make sure *you* did."

He wondered if she knew how lovely she looked when she smiled. Then he scoffed at the thought. Of course she did. She was a beautiful woman. They always knew stuff like that. Although she was married—he'd seen the diamond on her left hand—he found himself curious about his angel of mercy. "And who are you?"

"My name is Rachel Milligan." She brushed a wayward strand of blond hair back from her face with a slender hand. "I'm an emergency room nurse at Jackson Hole Memorial. I was in charge of the first-aid station today. I'm afraid my little girl is the one who beaned you."

"I didn't mean to do it."

The small voice came from his left. Ignoring the pain, Derek slowly turned his head in that direction. Rachel's daughter stood off to the side, anxiously shifting from one foot to the other.

Rachel gave the girl a reassuring smile. "This is Mickie."

"I'm really sorry, Mr. Rossi," the child said, drawing closer.

Derek guessed the girl to be nine, maybe ten. She was thin but not undernourished. Her face was covered in freckles and her eyes, instead of being blue like her mother's, were a vivid green, framed by thick brown lashes. But what Derek noticed most was her hair. It hung in long corkscrew curls halfway down her back. It was a tan color, not blond but not really brown either. She was cute, rather than pretty. He decided she must take after her father.

"I noticed a ball on the floor and I threw it to you." By now the child had tears in her eyes. "I didn't mean to hit you."

Before Derek could respond, the event coordinator returned juggling a cup of water and Tylenol in one hand and an ice pack in the other.

"Thanks, Ron." Derek swallowed the pills and pressed the ice bag gingerly against the side of his head.

Once that was done, he reflected on what the child had said, wondering if he'd heard correctly. The ball that had hit him had packed a wallop. Had it really been thrown by a *girl?*

"Do you forgive me?" By now tears were slipping down the girl's cheeks.

"Mr. Rossi understands it was an accident." The woman stared into his eyes. Her expression reminded him of a tigress protecting her young. "He's not angry with you."

Derek shrugged off Rachel's hold and rose to his feet. She quickly followed, standing close, as if worried he'd fall. For a second that seemed possible, but thankfully the spinning room righted itself.

"I'm not angry," he said. "I'm impressed."

Mickie cocked her head, clearly puzzled.

Rachel's jaw dropped. "Impressed?"

"Your kid has one mean throw." He shifted his attention to the child. "How long have you been playing ball?"

Mickie blinked. "Never. I just came here today to help Rachel."

"You call your mom Rachel?" Living in California, Derek knew lots of kids who called their parents by their first names. In fact, most of those moms and dads insisted on it. He just hadn't expected that to be the case in Jackson Hole.

"Rachel is my foster mom." The girl ducked her head and stared at her feet. "I'm just staying with her temporarily."

An armful of bats hit the hardwood and Derek jumped. A knifelike pain sliced his head open. He inhaled sharply.

"You're hurting." Ron stepped closer, his eyes filled with concern. "I think we should get you to a doctor—"

"I'm fine." Derek pressed the ice pack more firmly against his head and gestured to Rachel. "I have my own personal emergency room nurse."

"They don't come better than Rachel. She was on duty last year when they brought my son in." For a second the older man's eyes darkened, then he placed a fatherly hand on Derek's shoulders. "If you're still in pain next weekend, we can cancel your appointments."

"No way." Derek had made a commitment to do private lessons next Saturday and he honored his promises. Not to mention the proceeds were essential to Jackson Hole's fledgling Big Brothers Big Sisters program.

"At least promise you'll take care of yourself this week," Ron pressed.

Derek knew some guys might have been irritated by Ron's hovering. But the event coordinator had a big heart. Derek had seen that heart in the considerate way the gray-haired man had treated the kids and parents today.

"You got it," Derek said.

"Good." A look of relief crossed Ron's face. He removed his hand from Derek's shoulder and glanced at his watch.

"Go ahead and leave, Ron," Rachel urged. "I'll lock the doors."

"Closing up is my responsibility, not yours," Ron protested.

"Yes, but Amy Sue is expecting you at her piano recital. Your granddaughter will be disappointed if you don't show." Rachel's tone turned persuasive. "Besides, it will give me more time to observe Mr. Rossi before I clear him to drive home."

"Don't worry about me," Derek interrupted, annoyed at being discussed as if he wasn't in the room. "A couple hours and I guarantee I'll be good as new."

"See, Ron?" Rachel said. "Derek thinks you should go to the recital, too."

It wasn't exactly what he'd said, but Derek wasn't about to argue. Ron didn't need to hang around because of him.

The older man thought for a moment, then nodded. "You've convinced me."

Rachel breathed a sigh of relief. For a second she'd thought the older man might insist on staying. But family was important to Ron. After losing his son in a motorcycle accident last year, he'd made his loved ones even more of a priority. Still, instead of immediately hightailing it for the exit, the event coordinator turned back to Derek.

While the two men talked, Rachel stayed silent, listening, amazed at Derek's commitment to youth mentoring. It was a far cry from what she'd read and heard in the media recently. In fact, the tabloids had her believing the only thing Derek Rossi cared about was himself.

"Rachel, I'm hungry," Mickie whined when Ron finally strolled off. "When are we going to eat?"

"I'm a little hungry myself," Derek said.

Rachel turned. His eyes were blue, like hers. But while hers were just average run-of-the-mill blue, Derek's reminded her of the color of the ocean off a Caribbean island.

They were the eyes of a man who'd left a trail of broken hearts in his wake. Clean-shaven, with dark hair cut stylishly short, the former professional baseball player had a lean muscular build and a classic handsomeness that most women would find appealing.

She, on the other hand, preferred her men bigger, more rugged and bulky.

Like Tom.

Her heart gave a little ping.

"How about we all get something to eat?" Rachel said without thinking.

Derek's gaze turned speculative. "What about your husband? Will he join us?"

"I'm not married. Not anymore." Rachel spoke in the even tone she'd perfected the past three years. "My husband died."

Confusion clouded his eyes. "But you're wearing a wedding ring."

Rachel glanced at her left hand. Should she try to explain? He wouldn't get it. Even her friends didn't understand. How could they? They'd never had a husband murdered. Never kissed their spouse goodbye and had a sheriff show up less than an hour later with devastating news. They hadn't gone into early labor from the shock and been consumed by guilt because the baby, their long-awaited first child, had been too small to survive.

"Wearing it makes me feel like Tom is still with me, close by," she said unapologetically. "It probably sounds crazy to you—"

"Not at all," he said with such conviction that she almost believed him. "My father passed away from cancer when I was a little younger than Mickie. My mother wore her wedding ring until I was out of high school."

The empathy in his voice took her by surprise. And oddly, it made Rachel feel better to know another young widow had also sought comfort in the familiar….

"I *think* Rachel likes pizza," she heard Mickie say.

Rachel pulled her thoughts back to the present, wondering when the conversation had made the jump from rings to food. "Pizza is good."

"Great. Let's meet at Perfect Pizza." Derek turned and headed toward the door.

"Wait." Rachel hurried across the shiny hardwood after him, Mickie trailing behind her. "You shouldn't drive. Not yet."

He paused and turned. The hand holding the ice pack dropped to his side. "I told you, I'm fine. Once the Tylenol kicks in, I'll be ready to pitch a no-hitter."

Rachel couldn't keep her eyes off the large hematoma on the side of his head. This was her fault. She should have watched Mickie more closely, made sure the child didn't throw a ball to someone who wasn't looking.

"It's not your fault," he said softly as if he could read her mind. "Or anyone's fault. That's why they call 'em accidents."

He seemed quite sincere. Gracious as well as handsome. It was a potent combination. Rachel could see why women liked him.

"Seriously," he said. "I'm more than capable of driving myself."

The easy thing would be for her to agree. After all, he'd *probably* be okay. But then again, he'd taken a hard hit. He'd been confused and unsteady. No, she couldn't in good conscience let him get behind the wheel. Not yet, anyway.

"How about you humor me and ride with us over to the restaurant," she said. "Depending on how you're doing after we eat, you can either drive yourself home or I can drop you off."

Derek's quicksilver grin flashed. "You are bound and determined to get me in your car."

Although her heart skipped a beat, Rachel ignored the charm this guy seemed to have in abundance.

"I'm not going to let this drop." She resisted an unexpected urge to banter. "I don't want anything to happen to you on my watch."

His lips twitched. "Your watch?"

"Say yes," Mickie said, finally speaking up. "I want to eat."

Derek thought for a moment, then nodded, shifting his gaze to Rachel. "Ms. Milligan, you've got yourself a date."

A date? All she'd done was offer to drive him for pizza. Because they were hungry. Not because she wanted to get to know him better like you would if you were…dating…someone.

Rachel opened her mouth, then shut it. There was no point in getting hung up on semantics. They both knew it wasn't a date. After all, if the guy once voted "The Sexiest Player in the Major Leagues" was going to jump back into the dating game after his engagement scandal, it wouldn't be with her.

Chapter Two

Even though it was only five o'clock, Perfect Pizza was surprisingly busy. But Derek quickly located an empty table in the center of the small dining area.

He pulled out chairs for Mickie and Rachel, then took a seat opposite the two. After he was sure they were settled in, he snagged menus from the holder on the table and handed them each one. "What kind of pizza do you like?"

Mickie didn't even look at the menu in her hand. "Whatever you want is okay with me."

He'd noticed the child had done that a lot on the drive from the gym, refusing to offer an opinion, waiting to answer as if wanting to make sure her response was right. She was an odd bundle of energy and insecurity.

Derek fought the impulse to tease and lost. He'd grown up with a younger sister and Mickie reminded him of Sarah.

"How about anchovies, cream cheese and pineapple?" It was all Derek could do to keep a straight face at the look of horror that stole over the young girl's face.

"I think we'll pass on that combination." A tiny smile lifted the corners of Rachel's lips. She glanced at the menu and scooted closer to Mickie. "We can negotiate on the pineapple and cream cheese, but anchovies are definitely out. Right, Mickie?"

The child cast a look at Derek. What she saw must have reassured her because she nodded decisively and swiped the air with one hand. "Anchovies aaaaare out."

She sounded so much like an umpire that Derek had to laugh. After some friendly banter, they decided on a hamburger pizza with extra cheese. Rachel wanted him to stay at the table and rest, but he insisted on going to the counter to order.

While waiting in line, he glanced back at the table. Mickie was chattering on about something and Rachel gave the child her full attention. There was a look in the nurse's eyes that he hadn't noticed before. Sadness, yes. But also a longing that took his breath away.

This was a woman who obviously loved children. While her husband's death must have temporarily put an end to the dream of children of her own, he had no doubt kids were in her future. She was pretty and smart and personable. He was surprised she hadn't already remarried and started a family. Of course, wearing a wedding ring probably kept the decent men away.

Derek wondered if she'd consider him a decent guy. He certainly did his best to treat every woman with respect. That wasn't always the norm in today's society.

Lots of men out there had no scruples. Lots of women, too. An image of his former fiancée flashed before him. He clenched his jaw and focused on the menu board.

After ordering, Derek returned to the table with a pitcher of soda and three glasses filled with ice. "They'll bring out the pizza when it's ready."

In less than fifteen minutes a large golden brown pie oozing cheese appeared. After wolfing down three big pieces, Mickie spotted an old pinball machine in an alcove just off the dining room. Her eyes lit up. She smiled, showing a mouthful of big teeth.

"Want to check it out?" Derek asked.

The girl's smile faded. She lifted a shoulder in a slight shrug. "I don't know how to play."

He pushed back his chair and stood. "I'll show you."

After several pointers on how to best keep the silver ball in play, Derek gave her a handful of quarters and returned to the table. "She's a natural."

They chatted for a minute or two about Mickie and pinball machines before the conversation petered out. Rachel put down her second slice of pizza and sought for a comment to fill the lengthening silence. It had been easy to make conversation while Mickie was at the table, but now…

"Did you hear we have a seventy-percent chance of snow tomorrow?" Rachel asked.

Derek groaned out loud. "Please, no more about the weather or the bump on my head. We've talked those topics to death."

He was probably right. Perhaps she'd tried a little too hard to keep the conversation general. But when those brilliant blue eyes focused on her as if no one else in the world existed but the two of them, she felt as unsure as a fifteen-year-old on her first date.

Rachel placed her glass of soda on the wooden table with an unsteady hand. The man across from her had been to movie premieres. Partied with the beautiful people. And, according to the media, walked away from three engagements.

She glanced longingly at the door, wondering how she'd ever thought this was a good idea. Right now she could be at home in her PJs playing Scrabble with Mickie. Oh, Derek was nice. But she didn't like how he made her feel, all jittery and unsettled inside. "I'm a little nervous."

Derek lowered the glass he'd raised to his lips without drinking and Rachel wished she'd kept her mouth shut.

Disappointment filled his baby blues. "Which tabloids have you read?"

Rachel realized immediately that he'd misunderstood her comment. But the last thing she wanted was to discuss his troubles or her attraction to him. So instead, Rachel focused on the Derek Rossi she'd followed in the sports pages for almost a decade. "This will probably surprise you, but you and I go way back. I remember watching you pitch a no-hitter in the college world series. You were amazing. I followed your career after you were drafted by the Angels. Now it seems like every time I watch a sportscast, there you are with a microphone and an expert opinion."

His lips curved upward and Rachel, who'd planned to say even more, clamped her mouth shut. Dear God, what must he think? She'd been gushing like an out-of-control fan-girl.

"What have you heard recently?" he asked.

"I haven't been following your exploits in the tabloids," Rachel said. "If that's what you're asking."

"Still, I'm sure you've heard all about Niki and me."

She'd have had to be living in a cave *not* to have heard the news of his broken engagement to the young actress he'd been planning to marry last month, just before Thanksgiving.

She'd been disappointed that he would make such an important commitment, then walk away. Not just once, but three times. Still, it wasn't her place to judge. And she firmly believed it was better to walk away than say your vows to the wrong person. "Who you choose to marry, or not, is your own business."

The tiny lines of strain around Derek's eyes eased at her matter-of-fact tone. "No questions? No, how could you break it off only two weeks before the wedding?"

Would he tell her the truth if she asked? Rachel tamped down her curiosity. "Not my business. I'm sure you had your reasons."

"Thank you."

"But I am curious about one thing."

A resigned look crossed his face. "What's that?"

"How long do you plan to stay in Jackson Hole?"

A look of surprise skittered across his face. "That's the question?"

Rachel smiled.

"Not quite a month." Derek leaned back in his chair. "My buddy gave me the use of his vacation home just outside of Wilson until New Year's. Then I'll head back to L.A."

"Is that home?"

"For now." He took a sip of soda. "I'm originally from Minnesota. Most of my family still lives there."

Rachel relaxed against the back of her chair, enjoying the conversation. "I'm surprised you're not spending Christmas with them."

"If I'd married Niki, we'd still be on our honeymoon." His eyes took on a faraway look. Then he blinked and the moment was gone. "My sister and her family are spending the holidays with my brother-in-law's side of the family. My mother and Jim, her 'man-friend,' are in Florida visiting my aunt and uncle."

"I don't understand how you ended up in Wyoming."

"Great place to stay. Lots of good skiing. Best of all, no paparazzi." Derek grinned. "Feels like paradise to me."

Rachel picked up her half-eaten piece of pizza and took another bite, suddenly hungry.

"I've a question for you," he said.

Rachel forced the chunk of pizza past a sudden thickness in her throat. "Ask away."

"I've thought about doing foster care, but my schedule seems too chaotic to give a child the stability he or she needs." His eyes were bright with curiosity. "How do you make it work?"

Rachel leaned forward, resting her forearms on the table. Here was a topic she could discuss for hours. "I've had my license for a couple years. While a full-time placement wouldn't work with my schedule, I've done quite a bit of emergency foster care."

Although his eyes remained focused on her, he trailed a finger down the side of his glass. "Tell me more about that."

Rachel's mouth went dry. She swallowed, her heart fluttering in her throat. "An emergency placement can last anywhere from twenty-four hours to a month. Most kids I have for a day or two."

"How long will Mickie be with you?"

"Through the end of the month." Rachel shifted her gaze and let it linger on Mickie. Fingers on the side buttons, brows furrowed in concentration, her entire attention was on the game. It was typical Mickie. Her determined nature was only one of her many good qualities. Although the child hadn't even been under Rachel's roof a week, she'd already stolen her heart.

"Looks like she's made some friends."

Derek was right. The little girl had several new "friends" peering over her shoulders, watching her make the bells ding.

"Mickie is very social."

Derek could hear the pride in Rachel's voice. "What do you know about her history?"

Rachel thought for a moment. "I know her parents died in a car accident when she was five. After that she was sent to live with an aunt and uncle and four cousins. Several years later they divorced and relinquished Mickie, saying neither of them could afford to keep her."

Rachel's voice quivered. It had been hard losing her own parents when she'd been in college. But at least they'd been there while she was growing up and she had all those wonderful memories. Mickie had confided she barely remembered hers. And then to be turned out by the only family she had left…

Derek's eyes remained firmly fixed on her face. "What happened then?"

"Up until recently she's been living with a retired couple. Unfortunately their daughter has a chronic health condition that has worsened. They left for Arizona to be with her. According to the social worker they aren't planning to come back."

Rachel placed her glass of soda on the table and tried to ignore the butterflies in her stomach. She'd had men stare at her before, but when Derek gave her his full attention, it was overwhelming.

"What's going to happen to her once she leaves your place?" Derek asked, sounding truly concerned.

"The social worker told me they hope to have another home for her after the first of the year. If that doesn't pan out, she'll live in a group setting until one opens up."

Most people got a glazed look in their eyes when she talked about her foster kids. Not Derek. "I still don't understand how you can watch her and work full-time."

"I'm not working while she's with me," Rachel explained. "I had enough hours built up to take off the rest of the year."

His head cocked to one side. "You're taking vacation time to watch her?"

He made it sound as if she was making a big sacrifice when nothing could be farther from the truth.

"I don't have family here. My friends are understandably busy during the holidays with their husbands and children." Rachel lifted a shoulder in what she hoped was a casual shrug. "I find this time of year goes better for me if I keep busy. I love children, so having Mickie with me is the best way I can think of to spend my vacation. Trust me, it's a win-win situation for both of us."

Her eyes were clear and blue, her tone sincere. Even more revealing, she acted as if what she'd done was no big deal. Derek found himself not only impressed, but intrigued. Here was a woman he'd like to know better.

But he'd sworn off dating for the next six months. And no matter how lovely the woman, or how tempted he was to ask her out, there was no way he was breaking that pledge.

Chapter Three

Derek pulled the Escalade to the curb in front of a white clapboard house with green awnings. He turned off the engine. Although the sun had already gone down, and the moon wasn't particularly bright, the streetlight gave him a good view of the place. The home sat on a corner lot with big trees and a wide expanse of grass now covered with a thick blanket of snow. Lace curtains hung in front of the window and he could see people walking around inside, talking and laughing.

He turned off the engine but made no move to get out of the vehicle. Derek wasn't sure why he was here other than he was tired of his own company. After Rachel had dropped him off last Saturday night, he'd been mostly hanging out with, well, himself.

For several days he'd laid low, resting and keeping ice on the bump that had stuck out like a goose egg from his left temple. When she'd said goodbye, Rachel had handed him her phone number and told him to call if he had any questions. He'd reciprocated and given her his number. But she hadn't called. Neither had he.

Although he'd kept his phone close all weekend, Derek told himself he was relieved she hadn't contacted him. Not because he didn't like her, but because he did. Any other time he'd have asked her out on the spot. But this wasn't any other time. He'd just gotten out of a relationship that had taken him to the mat emotionally.

On his way to Jackson Hole he'd decided to take the next six months off from dating. He'd use the time to regroup, assess where he'd gone wrong and come up with a game plan for the future. That needed to be done before he jumped back into the dating pool.

Derek shoved the truck door open and stepped outside. That was why tonight was so perfect. Travis Fisher, a local he'd met while skiing at Jackson Hole today, had invited him to watch some college football bowl action with a group of his buddies. Travis had warned Derek that most of the guys were family men, so there'd be wives and kids present.

That didn't bother Derek. He was ready to get out of the house, but wasn't interested in hooking up. Football on the big screen, a couple of beers with the guys was all he was looking for this evening.

"Hey, Rach, could you get the appetizers out of the oven for me?" Mary Karen Vaughn appeared slightly frazzled as she grabbed a bag of chips from the cupboard.

"Absolutely," Rachel said in a cheerful tone, eager to be of help, happy she'd accepted Mary Karen's invitation.

She'd been so busy lately that she hadn't seen much of her friends.

There had been a few awkward moments initially. Like when Lexi Delacorte had asked if Derek Rossi was really as hot in person as he was on the television screen. The gleam in those amber eyes told Rachel her friend hoped the brief encounter with the sexy former baseball player had made her forget Tom. What Lexi didn't understand was that Rachel would never, could never, forget her husband.

The shy geologist she'd married just out of college may have been burly and taciturn on the outside, but he'd been sweet and sensitive inside. Her gentle giant. He'd been a fabulous husband. She had no doubt he'd have made a wonderful father...

A familiar pain stabbed her heart. No, it would be nearly impossible to find a man as good as Tom, which was why she hadn't even tried.

At least this holiday season she wouldn't need to worry about well-meaning friends trying to set her up. Normally, several times over Christmas there was someone's friend, cousin, uncle, coworker who was just *dying* to meet her.

This year all she had to concern herself with was making this the best Christmas ever for Mickie. Rachel's lips curved upward as she shut off the oven alarm, put on the bulky mitt and pulled out a baking sheet filled with the tiny almond-bacon cheese crostini she'd whipped up that morning. Reveling in the warmth against her face, Rachel inhaled the delicious aromas now flooding the kitchen.

"I should have made sure there wasn't a single college

bowl game on television before I set the date for this party," Mary Karen grumbled and slanted a glance at the men congregated in her living room.

"I like football." July Wahl added Fritos to an empty bowl and handed it to Mary Karen's five-year-old son, Connor. "But I don't really care who wins the Rotten Apple Bowl or whatever it is that's on TV tonight."

Rachel laughed. Mary Karen had thought her party was safe with a second-tier bowl on the tube. She'd quickly discovered otherwise.

"It could be called the Prune Bowl and my husband's eyes would still be glued to the screen." With dark hair that stopped just short of being black and amber eyes the color of topaz, Lexi Delacorte was the most beautiful of Rachel's friends. And the hospital social worker was as lovely on the inside as she was on the outside. "My Nick is a football fanatic."

A possessive pride filled Lexi's voice.

"I still can't believe you fell in love with a man who didn't know his own name." Mary Karen handed July a sheet of cheese sticks to put in the oven.

"I didn't need to know his name or that he loved football to recognize he was someone special." Lexi's eyes turned dreamy. "Or to fall hard for him."

"Two weddings in less than a year." July closed the oven door and straightened. Her speculative gaze settled on Mary Karen and Rachel. "You realize good things come in threes. That means one of you is next."

Rachel held up both hands, palms out, and shook her head.

Mary Karen laughed uproariously. "I have three little

boys to raise," she said when she could finally speak. "I don't need a fourth."

July chuckled, then fixed her gaze on Rachel. "Come on, Rach. Can't I interest you in a husband?"

"No husband for me." This was a discussion Rachel had had with her friends many times. Whenever they brought up the subject, she usually just laughed it off…or changed the subject. "But I will take a glass of wine."

Mary Karen lifted a half-empty bottle of merlot from the counter just as the doorbell rang. She paused, the bottle hovering over the glass. A frown furrowed her brows. "I wonder who that could be?"

"I'll go see." Rachel pulled off the bulky mitt and tossed it on the counter. "Just don't let anyone near my wine."

Rachel hurried past the living room full of cheering men and the family room where the kids sat watching a video. She waved at Mickie, wondering who else was coming. Although now that she thought about it, upon arrival Travis *had* mentioned something to her about inviting a guy he'd met skiing today. Pasting a smile of welcome on her face, Rachel opened the door.

She froze. Her breath caught in her throat. Standing on the porch was the last person she expected to see tonight. "Derek. Hello. It's…uh…good to see you."

Rachel couldn't stop the pleasure that sluiced through her at the sight of the man who'd consumed her thoughts the past five days. She told herself she was so happy because she'd been worried about him and was relieved to see him looking so…fabulous. Instead of being clouded with pain, his eyes were a clear blue. A slight bruising at his left temple seemed to be the only residual from the accident last week.

Yes, she was very happy he'd recovered so completely. Last weekend she'd picked up the phone five or six times to find out how he was doing. But each time she'd clicked off without placing the call, worried that after her fan-girl ramblings, he'd misinterpret the reason for the follow-up.

"This is a pleasant surprise." Derek's gaze slowly surveyed her from head to toe.

Rachel shivered. She reassured herself that the response had nothing to do with the heat in his eyes. It was simply because of the frigid temperatures. As if to further substantiate her explanation, the wind gusted, dusting his hair with white flakes and almost pulling the door from her hands.

"Come in, please." Rachel stepped back and motioned him inside. "It's freezing out there."

The second he was in the house, Rachel shut the door behind him. "I've wondered how you were doing."

"All you needed to do was call," he said in a teasing tone, his gaze never leaving her face. "You had my number."

Rachel wiped her sweaty palms against her jeans, battling unexpected butterflies. She smiled sweetly. "And you had mine."

"Touché." He chuckled and rocked back on his heels. "Well, it appears that despite our mutual lack of effort, our paths were meant to cross again."

"Looks that way." Suddenly Rachel was glad she'd chosen to wear her favorite blue sweater tonight, the one that matched her eyes. It gave her extra confidence to see the appreciation in Derek's gaze.

"Travis Fisher invited me." Derek glanced around as if expecting the man to materialize. Instead, a loud roar sounded from the living room. "Does he live here?"

Rachel could barely hear the question over the cheering in the other room.

"No, but you're at the right place," she said once the noise died down. Rachel gestured toward the living room. "Travis and the other guys are in there. Before you join them, let me take your coat."

Derek shrugged out of his jacket and handed it over, his hand brushing hers. His eyes darkened for a second as if he'd felt the same spark that shot up her arm.

Static electricity, she told herself. Simple static electricity.

"Is this your house?" His expression gave nothing away. It was almost as if they were polite strangers, which was what they were…right?

She clutched his coat tight against her. Still warm from the heat of his body, it retained the spicy scent of his cologne. "The house belongs to a friend of mine, Mary Karen Vaughn. She and Travis go way back."

"Do they live here together?"

Rachel couldn't help but laugh. "Oh, my goodness, no."

Everyone knew Mary Karen and Travis were tight. But living under the same roof with three small boys was a Travis impossibility.

"Derek, my man."

Travis's deep voice sounded behind her. "Glad you

could make it. Looks like you and Rachel are getting acquainted."

Derek smiled, relieved to see the man who'd invited him. And even more relieved to know Travis and Rachel weren't involved. "Actually, Rachel and I crossed paths last weekend at the Pitching and Catching Workshop."

"Really?" Travis turned to Rachel with a questioning glance. "I didn't know you liked base— Oof."

A small boy who looked to be about five years old slammed into Travis's side. A second boy who was the spitting image of the first—with the same mop of blond curls—immediately appeared. If not for the devilish gleam in their eyes, the two might have been mistaken for little angels.

"Mom needs your help," the one who'd done the initial body slam said to Travis.

The second boy shoved his twin hard, almost knocking him off his feet. "She told *me* to ask him."

"Enough." Derek stared in amazement as Travis grabbed both boys by the shoulder with firm hands and turned them around to face him.

"These two hellions are Connor and Caleb Vaughn." Travis's gaze shifted and his lips curved up in a smile. "That beautiful creature headed our way is their mother—and our hostess for the evening—Mary Karen."

The young woman looked more like a college student than a mother. Her blond hair was a little lighter than Rachel's and eyes weren't quite as blue. While her smile was warm and friendly, her eyes had a decidedly curious gleam. She held out her hand.

"Welcome. I'm Mary Karen Vaughn."

"Derek Rossi."

Her expression brightened. "You're the guy Mickie hit with a baseball."

"The girl has a wicked throw," Derek said, his smile widening at the memory. "But Rachel patched me up good as new."

Okay, so it was a bit of an exaggeration, but the pretty nurse *had* come to his rescue. And Derek had no doubt if there had been patching up to do, the woman standing to his right would have taken care of him.

During the five days since he'd last seen her, Derek had told himself she couldn't be nearly as beautiful as he remembered. But when she'd opened the door, he realized he'd been wrong. The blue of her sweater brought out the color of her eyes and her hair wasn't just blond, it was golden honey.

"Rachel is the best." Travis looped an arm around her shoulders.

Derek stiffened at the familiarity between the two. Had Rachel minimized her relationship with Travis? But he was almost certain Travis had also said he wasn't in a relationship. And where did Mary Karen fit into the picture?

"I wish I had a hundred Rachels," Travis added.

"Thank you for the compliment, Dr. Fisher." Rachel brought a finger to her lips, her eyes dancing. "But I think I've heard you give that same compliment to a dozen nurses in the past month."

"That's Travis." Mary Karen chuckled. "He's nothing if not consistent."

Derek felt the tension leave his shoulders at the warmth in her voice. Yes, there was definitely something going on with Travis. But whatever it was, it was between Mary Karen and the doctor.

Doctor?

Derek settled his gaze on Travis. "You're a physician?"

Travis tightened his grip on the squirming twins who were desperately trying to break free. "Yep. OB-GYN. It's a tough job, but someone has to do it."

"Don't let him fool you," Mary Karen said. "He loves the adoration."

"Mary Karen." A feminine voice rang out from the kitchen. "Could you come here, please?"

"Be right there," Mary Karen called out. She turned to go, then paused and refocused her attention on Derek. "Can I get you a beer? Or some wine?"

"A beer sounds good," Derek said. "I can get it myself if you just point me in the right direction."

Mary Karen smiled. "No worries. I can bring it to you."

"Connor said you needed me for something," Travis said before she walked away.

"It can wait," Mary Karen said with an airy wave. "Why don't you introduce Derek around?"

"After I drop his coat off in the bedroom, I'll start the sloppy joes." Rachel hugged Derek's jacket close and made her way to Mary Karen's bedroom at the back of the house, an extra spring in her step. Before Derek arrived she'd been having a perfectly fine time. But something about the former ball player brightened the cold winter night.

It had to be his smile. Derek Rossi loved life and it showed. Who wouldn't be drawn to a guy like that?

Rachel skidded to a stop. She wasn't attracted to Derek…was she? The woodsy scent of his cologne teased her nostrils and she realized not only did he look good, he smelled wonderful.

Not fair. Not fair at all.

Pressing her lips together, Rachel marched to the bed and threw his jacket on top of the other coats.

"He means nothing to me," she muttered.

"Are you okay?"

Rachel whirled. "Derek, what are you doing here? I mean, *here,* in the bedroom."

Even though her heart skipped rope in her chest, she relaxed her shoulders, determined to act casually. She only hoped the fire heating her cheeks didn't show.

Thankfully, he didn't appear to notice. He merely gestured to the bed with one hand. "I left my cell in my coat pocket."

Reaching past her, he retrieved the tiny phone and dropped it into his pocket. When he turned back, he was. Right. There. The large room suddenly seemed much too small.

"You look lovely tonight," he said.

A nervous chuckle slipped past Rachel's lips.

"I'm serious." His gaze darkened and the laughter died in her throat.

He was a mere heartbeat away and, without warning, Rachel found herself drowning in the deep blue of his eyes. She realized for the first time that there were tiny flecks of gold in the aquamarine depths. "You have beautiful eyes."

"So do you," he whispered.

Rachel wasn't sure who made the first move, but a

second later she found herself ensconced in Derek's arms...and she was kissing him.

The first few kisses were gentle ones, her mouth lightly brushing his. But that wasn't enough. She slid her fingers through his hair, pulling his mouth more tightly against hers. Although she hadn't kissed a man since Tom died, it felt so natural to be kissing Derek.

His tongue swept across her lips and she'd just opened her mouth to him when the door Derek had kicked shut flew open.

"The sloppy joes are—" Mary Karen stopped.

Rachel jerked out of Derek's arms.

"Derek came to get his cell phone." Her heart pounded and her breath came out in little puffs. "We got to talking and lost track of time."

A smile tugged at the corners of Mary Karen's lips. "I can have Lexi help me make the sloppy joes if you and Derek want to...*talk* some more."

Rachel kept her eyes focused on Mary Karen, trying to ignore the testosterone coming off Derek in waves. "We're done...talking."

"Sure you wouldn't rather stay here?" An impish smile lifted Mary Karen's lips. "You didn't look ready to conclude your *conversation*."

In that moment Rachel could see why David Wahl had accused his sister of making his life a living hell when they were growing up.

"I should get back and see how the game is going." Derek's gaze lingered on Rachel for several heartbeats before he finally left.

Mary Karen showed great restraint in remaining silent until Derek was out of earshot before she squealed,

"Ohmigod, you were practically doing it with the sexiest man in the major leagues."

"He's no longer playing ball." Rachel smoothed her hair with fingers that trembled slightly. "And may I point out, we were merely kissing."

"And may *I* point out that given a few minutes more, your clothes would have been on the floor."

Never. Kissing another man was bad enough. Making love would be unforgivable. Rachel crossed her arms. "You're wrong. I would never betray Tom like that."

Mary Karen's teasing smile faded. She placed a hand on Rachel's arm. "Honey, Tom is gone. You're still alive."

Rachel blinked back tears, appalled that not only had she kissed Derek, but she'd also *liked* it.

Mary Karen moved close, her blue eyes serious. "You deserve some happiness and I think this man may just be the one to give it to you. Think of him…as an early Christmas present. Unwrap him. Play with him. But most of all enjoy him. Something tells me he could give you some very pleasant memories."

Although Rachel had no doubt of that, she wasn't even tempted. Okay, maybe just a little. But while she liked Derek, her heart belonged to Tom. That was why this was one present that was going to stay wrapped.

Chapter Four

Mickie leaned back against the overstuffed sofa with a contented sigh. If Rachel hadn't agreed to take her in, she'd be spending the holidays in a group home. Instead she was here, surrounded by new friends.

She liked Mary Karen's house. Everything about it felt like a home. From the skinny Christmas tree decorated with strings of popcorn and dried cranberries to the tiny toy cars and plastic soldiers on the floor. When Mickie had first walked through the door she'd been a little scared. But then Addie, Lexi's daughter, had arrived with her family. They'd become instant friends.

"How long will you be staying with Rachel?" eight-year-old Addie asked.

"Until New Year's Day." Although she and Addie had lost interest in the movie after the first five minutes, the twins were still watching the DVD, so Mickie kept her voice low.

"That soon?" Addie's face fell. "I wish you were staying longer."

A familiar tightness gripped Mickie's heart. "I wish I could, too. Rachel is super nice."

In many ways the nurse reminded Mickie of her mother. Although she couldn't recall her mother's face, she remembered how she'd felt when her mom was alive. Safe. Loved. She felt that same way when she was with Rachel.

Addie twirled a strand of dark hair around her finger. "Maybe she could adopt you. Then you could stay."

As much as Mickie wished and prayed that would happen, it didn't seem likely. "Rachel said she'd like to keep me, but she works at the hospital and she's always gone."

"My mom works at the hospital," Addie said, a puzzled look on her face. "Up until she married Nick she had two jobs."

"Then it's an excuse." Tears pushed against the back of Mickie's lids. "She probably doesn't want me and is just saying she doesn't have enough time."

"Or maybe…" Addie's amber eyes lit up like a Christmas tree "…she thinks you need both a mom and a dad."

Mickie chewed on her lower lip. Rachel *had* told her more than once that she was sure there was a mommy and daddy out there for her somewhere. She hadn't just said a mommy. She'd said a mommy *and* a daddy. "You may be right. But while I'd like a dad, I really want Rachel to be my mom."

Addie's brows furrowed. "We have to find her a husband, like Nick. Only she can't have Nick because my mommy loves him. I love him, too."

Mickie fought back a pang of envy. "Rachel doesn't even have a boyfriend. And I'm leaving in three weeks."

"That's plenty of time," Addie said with a sureness that buoyed Mickie's spirits. "When my mommy met my stepdad, it only took a few days for them to be in love."

"Really?" If it took Addie's mother only a few days, surely Rachel could find someone in three weeks.

Addie's eyes took on a determined gleam. "We have to find a man who doesn't already have a wife. And he has to think Rachel is pretty. It won't work otherwise."

"Once we find this guy, how do we get them together?" Mickie felt silly asking a third-grader such grown-up stuff, but for being only eight, Addie knew an awful lot. Especially about moms and dads.

"You've got to get them to kiss." Addie picked up her Barbie and Ken dolls and pressed their faces together. "Like this."

"I saw Rachel kissing a guy in my mom's bedroom tonight," Connor said, not taking his eyes off the television screen.

Mickie was about to tell him he shouldn't be listening to a private conversation when the words registered. "Who was she kissing?"

"Was it Travis?" Addie asked, eyes full of excitement.

"Naw," Connor said, still not looking their way. "The new guy."

"That has to be Mr. Rossi," Mickie said. "He's really nice. Rachel and I went out for pizza with him once."

Addie dropped Barbie and Ken to the sofa, her eyes wide. "They've already been on a date?"

Mickie found Addie's excitement contagious. "I guess they have. And if they've already kissed…"

"I saw them," Connor said loudly.

"Connor sees everything," Addie said and Mickie could hear the admiration in her tone. Oh, yeah, Addie knew a lot.

"So what's the next step?" Mickie asked.

"They have to be together so they can do more kissing," Addie said. "Being together is veeeery important."

"That might be a problem." Mickie's heart sank. "Until tonight Rachel hasn't seen Mr. Rossi since last Saturday."

"You have to figure out a way," Addie said. "Otherwise they're not going to fall in love and you won't be able to stay here."

Mickie had tried being good and not asking for much because she'd wanted Rachel to like and hopefully keep her. That hadn't worked. Rachel liked her, but she was still sending her back.

Addie was right. Finding a husband for her temporary foster mom was her only chance. Mickie had to make Mr. Rossi and Rachel fall in love and get married. And she had less than a month to make that happen.

Although Addie's mom and stepdad had fallen in love in days, Mickie wasn't leaving anything to chance. She'd start right away. She had a lot riding on this and she couldn't afford to waste a single minute.

* * *

After the game ended at ten-thirty, Derek and the other guys left the big screen behind and wandered into the kitchen.

During the commercial breaks, Derek had learned a little bit about each of the men. David Wahl, an emergency room physician and Travis's longtime friend, was also Mary Karen's brother. Like Travis, David worked with Rachel at the local hospital. Nick Delacorte, Lexi's husband, was a partner at a law firm in Dallas. He and his family lived part of the year in Texas and the rest in Jackson Hole. And Travis, well, Derek had been shocked to learn that the young doctor had helped raise seven younger siblings. No wonder he was in no hurry to settle down.

He'd enjoyed watching the game with them. The beer had been cold, the appetizers unending and the high-def television had surround sound so he could hear every hit. The only downside to the evening had been the incident with Rachel. Although he knew she'd deny it, he'd taken advantage of her. Just because she'd kissed him first didn't mean he had to respond so enthusiastically.

She'd barely spoken to him since. Even when she'd put the sloppy joe on his plate, she'd only said a few words to him.

Despite her attempt at a freeze-out, when he entered the kitchen he looked for her. He found her at the counter, back to him, adding ground beans to the coffeemaker.

"Would you like a brownie with ice cream?" Lexi gestured to the plate of chocolate squares on the counter in front of her.

Derek hesitated. They looked delicious, but he'd eaten two sloppy joes and way too many appetizers while watching the game. Still, he did like chocolate….

"Don't worry," a small voice said. "My mommy made them herself. They're super good."

Even though there seemed to be a gazillion kids running around the house tonight, he immediately made the connection. It wasn't difficult. The child was the spitting image of her mother. "You must be Lexi's daughter."

"That's right. I'm Addie." The child slanted a sideways glance at Mickie, who'd just walked up. "He's smart. I like him."

Mickie's cheeks turned a bright red. "How did you like the football game?"

"It was okay." Derek elbowed Travis in the side. "Though the company left a lot to be desired."

"Hey, any more talk like that and we won't invite you back," Travis shot back.

"I think I may have something to say about that." Mary Karen chuckled. "This is my house after all."

Mickie stiffened and exchanged a worried glance with Addie.

"It's okay." Derek placed a reassuring hand on Mickie's shoulder. "We're just joking."

"Why don't you girls grab some dessert and take it over there." Mary Karen gestured with her head to a card table in the corner of the kitchen. The boys had been put to bed, but Addie and Mickie had been allowed to stay up.

Carefully balancing her dessert, Addie made her way to the table, but Mickie stayed put, her gaze firmly fixed on Derek. "I have something to ask you."

Mickie looked so serious, the teasing words he'd been about to say died on his tongue. "What is it?"

She took a deep breath. "You're giving private pitching lessons this Saturday, right?"

"I am." He wondered how she knew, then remembered the topic coming up when everyone was getting their food earlier.

"Will you give me a lesson?"

She looked so earnest, he hated to turn her down, but he didn't have a choice. "I'd love to, sweetheart," he said. "But I'm afraid all the slots are filled."

A stricken look crossed the child's face. "Please. You said I had a good arm." She clasped her hands together and lifted them as if praying. "I'm not good at anything, but I'd like to be. Can't you please help me? Pretty please."

"Mickie, Mr. Rossi said no," Rachel said from across the room, her voice firm but gentle.

The girl's shoulders dropped. Her bottom lip trembled. The look on her face said he'd dashed a lifelong dream by not giving her a private lesson. He thought for a moment, considering the options. "Come around noon. All the appointments will be over by then."

"Derek, you don't have to do that," Rachel said.

He smiled, feeling his spirits lift. At least Rachel was talking to him now. He placed a hand on Mickie's shoulder. "I like helping aspiring ballplayers."

"Afterward you can come to Rachel's house and have lunch with us." The words tumbled from Mickie's lips, one word chasing the other. "You can meet Fred, Rachel's bloodhound. He's super sweet. He—"

"Mickie," Rachel interrupted. "I'm sure Mr. Rossi has better things to do."

"Actually, I don't." Even if he had, Derek would have changed them. The pleading look in the girl's eyes tugged at his heartstrings. He shifted his gaze to Rachel. "Unless you have other plans?"

For the first time he was aware of other eyes on them. *Let them stare,* he thought. There was only one person's response he cared about.

"No." Rachel reached behind her and pushed the start on the coffeemaker, her cheeks a becoming pink. "No plans."

"Great." He exhaled the breath he didn't know he'd been holding. "I'll see you both at noon on Saturday."

"Thank you so much." Mickie wrapped her arms around his waist in a quick hug, then headed to the card table until Lexi called her back for her brownie.

When Lexi handed him a plate filled with ice cream and a large brownie square, Derek didn't have the heart to refuse.

"You made Mickie's night." Rachel took the plate of dessert that her friend pushed into her hands, then slipped past Derek to take a seat at the dining-room table.

"It seemed to mean a lot to her." Derek commandeered the seat next to her, placing his plate on the table.

"Until tonight I had no idea Mickie was so interested in sports," Rachel mused, picking up her fork.

"It takes time to get to know someone." Derek couldn't help thinking of Niki and how long it had taken before he'd seen her true colors. "Perhaps she's just now feeling comfortable enough to share more about herself with you."

Rachel forked off a piece of brownie. "Perhaps."

"I didn't know you had a bloodhound," he said, wanting the conversation to continue. "I grew up with one. We called him Gus."

"Cute name," Rachel said.

Derek wasn't sure about the name being "cute," but it had fit the dog.

"A lot of people think it's crazy for me to have an animal that big when I live in a condo," she continued. "But once I saw him, I couldn't imagine getting a different breed."

"I can't wait to meet him." Okay, so they were talking about a dog. At least they were talking.

"He'll be excited to see you," Rachel said.

Will you *be excited to see me?* Instead of asking, Derek took a bite of brownie and reminded himself that Saturday wasn't about him and Rachel; it was about Mickie. He needed to keep that in mind before he did something he'd regret.

Something like forgetting he was supposed to be girlfriend-free for the next six months.

"I'm ready to go." Mickie twirled around in Rachel's small living room, while Fred sat in the doorway watching her.

Rachel smiled. Addie loved to twirl and had shown Mickie how it was done when they'd been at Mary Karen's house.

"Honey, it's only eleven." Rachel glanced down at her watch just to be sure. "Eleven-oh-six to be exact. It takes less than ten minutes to get there. Besides, I still have some picking up to do."

Although Rachel normally kept her apartment spic and span, this week she and Mickie had done more socializing than cleaning.

"I understand." Mickie stopped twirling long enough to kiss the top of Fred's head. "You don't want Mr. Rossi to think you live in a pigsty."

Rachel chuckled. "Do you even know what a pigsty is?"

"A messy house," Mickie said promptly. "That's what the social workers always called my aunt and uncle's home. But their place was a zillion times worse."

"Thanks." Rachel scooped up a newspaper she'd left on the sofa. "I guess."

She couldn't believe Derek was coming over for lunch. If Mickie hadn't arranged the lesson, Rachel doubted she'd have seen him again.

Her lips quirked up in a wry smile. Of course, given her luck, their paths would have crossed again.

"Do you like Mr. Rossi?" Mickie called out, mid-twirl.

Rachel paused, dust cloth in hand. "He seems like a good guy. Why do you ask?"

"When we were at the sports facility, you were nice to him." Mickie stopped twirling. "But not at Mrs. Vaughn's home."

Rachel pulled her brows together. Surely that wasn't true. She'd been embarrassed by her behavior in the bedroom, but that whole incident had been her fault, not his.

"You acted like you hated him," Mickie continued. "I could tell it made him feel bad."

Rachel's heart dropped. "You think so?"

Mickie nodded with such decisiveness that Rachel's heart dropped even lower. "Maybe if you're extra nice to him today he'll know you don't hate him."

"That's a good idea."

The child smiled and once again began to twirl.

Chapter Five

Derek had been so focused on showing a young boy how to throw a slider that he couldn't say for sure when Rachel and Mickie had entered the Indoor Sports Facility. All he knew was when the boy and his dad walked off, he caught sight of them leaning against the wall.

When he met Rachel's gaze she surprised him with a friendly smile. After the kisses in the bedroom, the interaction between them had been strained and he'd worried he'd damaged their budding friendship.

He returned Mickie's wave and made his way across the gym floor, hoping all was forgiven and forgotten. He really would like to be Rachel's friend.

"Hi, there!" he called out as he drew close.

"Good morning," Rachel said, then glanced up at the large clock on the wall. "Or rather, good afternoon."

"Hi, Mr. Rossi." Mickie hurried to his side with a speed that surprised him. Once there, she tugged on his sleeve. "Don't forget you're coming for lunch. We're having grilled cheese sandwiches."

For a second Derek got the impression that the child was more excited about the lunch than the lesson. But that was crazy.

"I haven't forgotten." He shot her a reassuring smile. "Lunch. After the lesson."

"I'm curious." Rachel glanced around the gym. "Since Mickie has never played before, where do you begin?"

Today Rachel had pulled her hair back in a ponytail and dressed simply in jeans, a red sweater with silver threads and sneakers. Even though she didn't appear to be wearing makeup, she had to be because her lips were almost as red as her sweater. He couldn't help remembering how sweet those lips had tasted.

With great effort Derek pulled his attention back to the matter at hand. "We start with the basics. Like how to grip a ball. Then, I thought she could throw the ball to you while I coach her on her stance and technique."

"I don't have anything to put on my hand." Mickie raised her left arm and wiggled her fingers as if showing off her bright pink polish.

Derek tilted his head. Sometimes little girls could be very confusing creatures.

"She doesn't have a glove," Rachel clarified. "We were running late and by the time I remembered, we were almost here."

"Rachel had to make sure the house was clean for you," Mickie added.

Derek swore he heard Rachel groan. He hid a smile.

"I'm so sorry," Rachel said. "Here you go out of your way to help and—"

"No worries." Derek lifted his hand in a dismissive wave. "We have plenty of gloves kicking around here. And she's not the only one who'll need one. Because Mickie will be throwing to you, you'll need one as well."

"Me?" Rachel's voice rose, then cracked. "I haven't had a glove on since college. And that was only intramural softball."

"You'll do fine," Derek said. "After all, today is all about learning and having fun."

Rachel reminded herself that she was throwing a ball to a ten-year-old, not trying out for the major leagues. "All right, then. Let's play ball."

He shot Rachel and approving smile, then refocused on Mickie.

"Lesson number one." Derek held up the ball in his hand. "The best way to grip a ball is across the seams."

He held it out so both Mickie and Rachel could see. "And when you hold it, try to keep the ball out on your fingertips, not up against your palm."

"Why?" Mickie asked as he flipped the ball to her.

The girl caught the ball easily, but struggled to get a good grip.

"Holding it the proper way helps your speed and accuracy when you throw," he said.

Derek stepped forward, positioned the ball in Mickie's hand, then ran backward while slipping on his glove. He punched the pocket with his fist. "Throw it here."

She lifted her hand and with a stiff arm tossed it to him. It went far to his left, but he easily snagged it.

"Good effort." He moved to her side and showed her how to cock her wrist back and use it as part of the throwing motion.

Once the girl had a good start on that skill, he gave both of them gloves and had Mickie throw the ball to Rachel. While the child threw, Derek coached her on her stance.

Thankfully Rachel had no problems catching the balls. Mickie improved with each throw and showed definite potential. Oddly, she seemed more interested in talking about all of Rachel's wonderful attributes than in paying attention to her throwing technique.

"My stomach is growling," Mickie said when only a half hour had passed.

Derek motioned to Rachel.

"Mickie is hungry," he said when she drew close.

"Mr. Rossi is hungry, too," Mickie protested.

"You're right." He smiled at the child. "I am."

"How does grilled cheese sandwiches and tomato basil soup sound?" Rachel asked. "Be honest. We want you to be happy."

For a second he was tempted to tell her he could simply sit and look at her and be happy, but that sounded too much like a come-on.

"Soup and a sandwich works for me," Derek said. "But it sounds like you've been busy cleaning all morning. I hate to make you go to more work."

"She doesn't mind," Mickie said before Rachel could answer. "You showed me a lot. Plus you have to meet Fred. I told him all about you."

Derek grinned. Apparently his family wasn't the only one where the dog wasn't simply a pet but rather a member of the family.

"I wrote down my address." Rachel reached into her pocket and pulled out a piece of paper. "Do you need directions? I know getting around Jackson Hole can be confusing."

Derek glanced at the sheet, then shoved it into his pocket. "Thanks, but no directions are necessary. I'll just plug your address into my GPS."

Out of the corner of his eyes, Derek saw Mickie wander over to the sports locker to put away the gloves and balls. This gave him the opportunity he'd been waiting for.

"In case you're concerned, I want you to know that you don't have a thing to worry about." At the confused look on her pretty face, he stopped and reconsidered. Had she put it out of her mind? Was he dredging up the past for no reason?

Unfortunately he'd said too much already to take it back.

Rachel's brows furrowed. "I don't understand."

"The kissing. I was out of line."

"But *I* was the one who kissed *you*," Rachel said.

"That's not how I remember it."

"It doesn't matter." She took a step closer and the scent of vanilla surrounded him. "It was a freak occurrence that I'm sure neither of us wants to repeat."

What? She considered kissing him to be a *freaky* thing?

His shock must have shown on his face because she grimaced. "That didn't come out quite right."

"I understand," he said. *I think*.

But he didn't. How could she dismiss what they'd shared? Even if the kiss had been ill-conceived, the connection between them had been unbelievable. Derek's gaze slid to her lips. Not only did she have a beautiful face, but she also had really lovely lips. Full and plump, like ripe strawberries. And he'd already discovered that her mouth tasted as good as it looked.

His body began to stir, but he reminded himself he was supposed to be figuring out what went wrong with his previous relationships, not getting all hot and bothered. Or doing any *freaky* kissing. Derek had almost ruined his friendship with this beautiful woman by going down the physical road.

He wasn't about to make that mistake again. No matter how many cold showers he had to take.

The planned development just south of Jackson was a charming mixture of single-family houses, townhomes and apartment complexes. With the help of his GPS, Derek easily found Rachel's townhome at the easternmost edge. A gravel road ran down the side of her property separating the development from a field that stretched far into the distance.

Derek parked at the curb and stepped outside. Although the wind had a sharp edge, he paused when he reached the sidewalk and took a deep breath. The wide-open spaces of this beautiful state and the clean crisp air reminded him of Minnesota. Over the years he'd adjusted to life in Los Angeles, but he still missed the change of seasons and being able to look into the distance without seeing a bunch of buildings.

"Derek, come inside. It's cold out there."

He pulled his gaze from the scenic vista to settle on something even more stunning. Rachel stood in the doorway, her wheat-colored hair blowing softly about her face, a welcoming smile on her lips. Derek's hopes rose. Maybe their talk had cleared the air. Maybe the kiss—or rather his behavior during the kiss—had been forgiven or, better yet, forgotten.

Mickie peered around Rachel's side. "Hurry. Fred and the grilled cheese sandwiches are waiting."

Derek brushed the snowflakes from his face and hustled up the driveway.

He hadn't realized how cold it was until he stepped inside and the warmth surrounded him. While Rachel hung up his coat and Mickie scampered off to bring Fred in from the backyard, Derek took the opportunity to look around.

An open floor plan enhanced the modest space. A small entry gave way to a fair-size living room decorated in tans and browns with burgundy accents. Farther back was a kitchen and dining area. Off to his right was a hallway he assumed led to the bedrooms.

While more modern than Mary Karen's house, it still had the same homey feel. He couldn't help but be curious. Had Rachel shared this home with her husband?

"You have a nice place." He shoved his hands into his pockets and rocked back on his heels. "Looks new."

"Fairly new," Rachel said. "I moved in right after it was built. I'll be here three years come March."

Which meant she hadn't lived here with Tom. For some reason, the knowledge pleased him.

"Let me get you something to drink." Rachel moved

toward the kitchen bypassing an oval-shaped wooden table decorated with red-and-green plaid place mats and Santa napkin rings.

Derek started to follow, but a photograph on a side table caught his eye and stopped him in his tracks. It was obviously a wedding picture. A much-younger Rachel dressed in a simple white wedding gown smiled up at a large mountain of a man with sandy hair and a full beard. The photographer had captured the love in her eyes and amazingly, despite Tom's solemn expression, in his as well.

Oddly, the picture made Derek feel better. Better about three broken engagements. Better about being single. Despite the bad press, he'd been right to walk away from his former fiancées. Not one of those women had looked at him the way Rachel had looked at her husband.

"Derek." Rachel's voice broke through his thoughts. "What would you like to drink? Soda? Milk? Or something hot?"

He pulled his gaze away from the portrait. "Milk, please."

The sound of the back door slamming shut echoed throughout the house. Derek heard Mickie's voice, but it took a few seconds before the girl joined them, a large red-and-black bloodhound at her side.

"Don't worry, I wiped his feet off," Mickie said when Rachel's gaze dropped to the large paws.

"Good job." Approval ran through Rachel's voice like warm honey and Mickie puffed with pride at the praise.

Derek studied the dog. Although Gus had been more

tan than red, Fred still brought the memories of his childhood friend surging forth. Gus licking his face after his father died. Gus's comforting warmth next to him in bed at night. Gus at his heels, following him everywhere. The way Fred was glued to Mickie's side, the two hounds were obviously cut from the same cloth. "So, this is your Fred."

"He's actually Rachel's dog," Mickie said, her tone wistful. Fred nudged her hand with his snout and the smile returned to her face. Mickie scratched his head.

"He's a super good boy." Mickie met Derek's gaze. "He knows lots of tricks. Want to see?"

Derek nodded, eager to see what the animal could do. While a great companion, Gus had never been particularly good with tricks.

"Fred, sit," Mickie said in a firm tone.

The dog was already sitting.

"Fred, shake," Mickie ordered.

The dog tilted his big head and looked up at him.

"Go ahead," Mickie said to Derek. "Shake his paw."

Derek squatted down, lifted the paw that had been firmly planted on the floor and while gazing into the soulful eyes, shook it with enthusiasm. "Hello, Fred. I'm Derek. It's nice to meet you."

"Fred, kiss."

Before Derek could react the dog leaned forward and slurped his tongue along his cheek.

Derek grinned and ruffled the loose skin around the dog's neck. Figured he'd get that one right. "You remind me of Gus."

Fred thumped his tail against the hardwood floor as if he knew that was a very good thing.

"Honey, could you show Derek where he can wash his hands?" Rachel flipped the sandwiches off the griddle and onto three plates. "By the time you get back, lunch should be on the table."

He followed Mickie to a bathroom with soap in the shape of Christmas trees and frilly towels that seemed more decorative than serviceable. After washing his hands, he hesitated. But Mickie confided that while they seemed too pretty to use, Rachel had been offended when she'd used toilet paper to dry her hands.

Still he hesitated.

With a conspiratorial smile, Mickie pulled off some toilet paper and handed some to him and kept the rest for herself. After they finished drying their hands, Derek added Mickie's toilet paper to his own and flushed away the evidence.

By the time they returned to the kitchen, Mickie had stopped giggling. Fred was on the floor next to the sofa sleeping and Rachel was filling the glasses with milk.

After pulling out the chairs for both Rachel and Mickie, Derek took a seat, dropping the napkin onto his lap. "Smells good."

He waited for Rachel to pick up her spoon. Instead, she asked him to say grace. It wasn't that difficult a request, but for a second Derek went blank. Although he'd grown up praying before meals and going to church, since he'd moved away from home at eighteen he could count on one hand the times he'd done either.

"Say what you're thankful for and then thank God for

the food," Mickie said in a whisper so loud she might as well have spoken in her normal tone.

Even with her head bowed, Derek could see Rachel smile.

He took a deep breath. "Thank You, God, for not only this wonderful food but also for bringing Rachel and Mickie into my life. Amen."

Derek realized as he said the words that they weren't just the "right" thing to say, he meant them.

The perfectly seasoned soup was delicious. The grilled sandwich made with three cheeses, the best he'd ever eaten. And unlike the afternoon at the pizza place, the conversation flowed easily.

Over lunch he and Rachel talked about everything from her volunteer work at a local free clinic to his current dilemma—whether to renew his lease on his L.A. apartment or look for a new place to live. Derek let his gaze linger on her face. Her skin was smooth and creamy and her eyes reminded him of the Wyoming sky. She'd ditched the ponytail from this morning and her golden blond hair now hung loose to her shoulders.

She was amazing. Not only was she beautiful, she appeared to have it all together while he felt as if he'd let his life stray off course. Not just in relation to his faith but also in his commitment to his family. He loved his mother and sister, but he'd let weeks go by without calling them. "Have you ever looked at your life and wondered if you'd taken a wrong turn somewhere?"

Rachel's eyes widened and Derek realized he'd spoken aloud. He was trying to figure out how to call the words back when Mickie answered.

"I turned the wrong way once when I lived with my

aunt and uncle." Her voice which had started off strong unexpectedly began to tremble. She twisted a strand of hair around one finger, her green eyes clouded. "By the time I finally got home it was dark. I was really scared. Aunt Amy was worried, but Uncle Wayne was mad. She wouldn't let him go bowling until she knew I was safe."

The pain in the child's voice told Derek everything. He could only imagine how "Uncle Wayne" had treated the child once she'd gotten home. He tightened his fingers around his soup spoon.

"I hadn't lived there long, but I knew what happened when you made Uncle Wayne mad," Mickie said. "Especially when he was drinking beer. And he was always drinking beer."

Silence descended over the table for several heartbeats.

"Did he hit you?" Rachel asked finally.

Mickie lifted a shoulder, then let it drop. "Sometimes."

Fred, who'd been lying on the floor at Mickie's feet, sat up. Without looking down she scratched his head.

The muscle jumping in Rachel's jaw told Derek exactly what she'd like to do to Uncle Wayne.

He understood. He felt the same way. Although he'd seen it often enough in his role as a Big Brother, the harming of a child never went down easy. He shoved down the rage rising inside him and forced a casual tone. "I'm sorry that happened to you."

He placed his spoon on the table and took an unfrosted sugar cookie from the plate in the center of the table. He broke it into two pieces, handed one to Mickie and kept the other for himself. "He shouldn't have hit you."

Mickie took a bite of cookie. "I know lots of kids who get hit."

Derek winced. Yeah, he did, too.

"That won't happen here," Rachel said softly. "You're safe with me."

Mickie crumbled the rest of the cookie between her fingers. "What if I say or do something that makes you mad?"

"It doesn't matter," Rachel said, her eyes filled with compassion. "An adult should *never* hit a child. For any reason, but especially not out of anger."

Derek remained silent. This conversation was between mother and daughter, er, between Rachel and Mickie.

"Do you understand?" Rachel covered the girl's hand with hers.

Mickie nodded her head in several quick jerks.

"And I want you to know you can be honest with me about your feelings," she continued.

The child's face scrunched into a frown. "I don't... understand."

"Just tell me what you want when I ask," Rachel said.

"In other words, if you don't like anchovies, it's okay to say you don't like them," Derek clarified.

"If you're worried or afraid, I want to know that, too." Rachel grabbed a cookie and absently took a bite. "I can't make something better unless I know it's an issue."

Derek took another cookie. These were even better

than the ones his mother made every Christmas. In fact, they were the best he'd had in years. He caught Mickie staring as he popped half the cookie into his mouth.

"Okay, I understand." Mickie's gaze shifted back to Rachel. "But can we decorate the cookies before you and Mr. Rossi eat them all?"

Rachel chuckled.

Derek grinned.

Mickie giggled.

Fred woofed.

And in the cozy kitchen, with the light streaming through the windows, for the first time in years, Derek felt part of a family.

Chapter Six

Rachel had expected Derek to leave immediately after lunch. In fact, when he'd first arrived, she'd thought of several excuses, er, reasons, to make sure that happened. She'd been concerned that he would misconstrue her generosity and think she was interested in him.

But he'd been a perfect gentleman and they'd been having such a good time that she'd impulsively asked him to stay and decorate sugar cookies with her and Mickie. Even though applying frosting and sprinkles was more of a "girly" thing to do, she'd been confident he'd say yes. After all, from how many he'd eaten it was apparent he loved her cookies. She'd been shocked when he'd begged off with some pitiful excuse about needing to talk with his agent.

Rachel wasn't sure who was more disappointed—her, Mickie or…Fred. The animal had taken a shine to Derek and now sat staring at the door long after the man had walked through it.

"I wish Mr. Rossi could have stayed." Mickie crooked her elbow on the table and rested her chin on her hand.

"Me, too." Rachel forced an upbeat tone. "But you and I'll have fun, just the two of us."

Mickie kicked at table leg. "I guess."

Rachel thought for a minute. "How about I see if Addie and Lexi can come over and help us decorate these cookies?"

Mickie's eyes lit up. She straightened in her seat. "That would be fantabulous. I need to talk to Addie anyway."

Rachel had pulled out her cell phone, but now paused before flipping open the cover. What could Mickie possibly need to speak with Addie about? "Is it anything I could answer? Or help with?"

"It's nothing important." Mickie avoided Rachel's eyes. "Addie knows I don't have many toys and she loaned me her Barbie and Ken. Last night I had them go on a date. I need to ask her what comes next."

Rachel's heart went out to the young girl. With her parents dying so young and her aunt and uncle being less-than-stellar role models, Mickie probably didn't have a clue how men and women *should* interact. "Do you want them to fall in love?"

"Of course." Mickie sounded shocked she'd even asked.

"I'd say another date comes next," Rachel said. "If Barbie and Ken are going to fall in love and—"

"Get married," Mickie said, completing the sentence.

"Right." Rachel hid a smile. Who knew the little girl was such a romantic? "Well, then, the two need to spend time together."

"That's what Addie said."

"Addie is correct."

Mickie chewed on her lower lip. "Do they *have* to go on a date?"

Rachel thought back to her own dating years. "When Tom and I were getting to know each other, some of my fondest memories are when we simply hung out and talked."

"Then you fell in love and got married, right?"

"We did," Rachel said. "But some couples discover after spending a lot of time together that they don't work, that they're not really meant for each other."

"They *are* meant for each other. And they have to fall in love," Mickie said with a vehemence that took Rachel by surprise. "Ken thinks Barbie is pretty and she thinks he's handsome. I don't see why they wouldn't get together, do you?"

Rachel opened her mouth to tell Mickie that it takes a lot more than physical attraction to make a relationship work, but reconsidered at the last minute. These were dolls they were talking about, not real people.

With that thought firmly planted in her head, Rachel smiled and leaned forward. She gently pushed a strand of hair back from Mickie's face with her fingertips. "With you doing the matchmaking, I firmly believe your two are destined to walk down the aisle."

A look of pure joy filled the young girl's eyes. Before

Rachel knew what was happening, Mickie jumped out of her seat and flung her arms around Rachel's neck. "I think so, too."

Rachel wrapped her arms around the child and returned the hug, unexpected tears stinging her eyes.

When she'd agreed to care for Mickie, she thought she'd be able to bring the little girl into her life for thirty days and then let her go. But now, that seemed an impossible task. Knowing and loving this child as she did, Rachel couldn't imagine letting Mickie walk out of her life…ever.

Mickie sat in the hard wooden pew and watched the families slowly file into the church. Hope rose in her chest. Very soon she'd have a mommy and a daddy, too. That was, if God didn't strike her dead first.

She hated having all this time to think. Hated having all this time to worry about God being angry with her. They'd arrived early and Rachel had told her to take this time to talk to God.

The trouble was, God probably didn't want to hear from her, especially not after what she'd done. Still, if God really did know everything—like Rachel said he did—surely he knew how important it was that Rachel and Mr. Rossi got together. And really, if Rachel had thought about it, she'd have emailed Mr. Rossi and invited him to church herself. So, when Mickie used Rachel's private email address to ask Mr. Rossi to come this morning, it was almost as if she was doing everyone a favor.

"Is he here yet?" Addie whispered in her ear.

"Do you see him sitting with us?" Mickie's whisper

held a sharp edge. But darn it, Addie had made her believe it was possible to get Mr. Rossi there. But with only five minutes left before church started, it looked like he would be a no-show.

"There's still time," Addie said in her ear. "Pray harder."

Mickie obligingly screwed her eyes shut and clasped her hands tight together. *Dear God, please let Mr. Rossi come. Please let Mr. Rossi come. Please let Mr. Rossi*—

"Is this seat taken?" a familiar deep voice asked.

Mickie opened her eyes. Her lips curved into a relieved smile. It looked as if her prayers had been answered after all.

Derek stood at the edge of the pew, his confidence slipping away with each passing heartbeat. When he'd checked his email this morning he'd been shocked to see one from Rachel. They'd all been discussing email addresses at Mary Karen's house and he'd mentioned what his was in passing. He hadn't expected her to remember it or to send him an invitation to attend church with her and Mickie.

The way she was looking at him now told him she'd never expected him to show.

Uncharacteristically nervous, he shifted from one foot to the other. "If it's too crowded…"

"There's plenty of room." Mickie leaned across Rachel and motioned for him to enter the pew.

"Yes, there's more than enough room." Rachel slid closer to Mickie.

"Hi, Mr. Rossi." The girl's green eyes sparkled like

emeralds. He'd never seen a child so happy to be in church.

"Good morning." He returned her smile and settled in next to Rachel.

"I didn't expect to—" Rachel began, but then the organ wheezed and the congregation rose. She held out the hymnal so they could share.

While they sang, he slanted a sideways glance at her, marveling at her beauty. Today she had on a fluffy blue sweater and a black skirt. Her hair hung to her shoulders in soft curls and she smelled as good as he looked. Derek forced his attention back to the hymn and realized their voices blended with such ease that it was as if they'd been singing together for years.

Even though there was no chance to talk, it felt good simply being next to her. He might not have known her long, but he felt comfortable around her, and comfortable being back in church.

He was glad he'd accepted her invitation. And to think he'd almost blown her off. But then, he'd reminded himself that he wanted to get back into the habit of regular worship. Still, that hadn't been the deciding factor. It had been the last line of her email that had made it difficult for him to stay away.

I'd really like to see you again.

Rachel was so private about her feelings that he knew it must have taken a lot for her to add that to the email. He worried that if he didn't show up, she might take his absence personally.

No, he had to be here. The last thing he wanted to do was disappoint this lovely lady.

He stopped singing for a second and leaned close, his lips brushing her ear. "I'm glad I came."

She turned, her cheeks a bright pink, her eyes a breathtaking blue. "I'm happy you did, too."

From that moment on, Rachel had difficulty keeping her mind on all things God. Like right now, she was trying to listen to the sermon, but how could she concentrate with Derek's muscular thigh pressed so tightly against her leg?

Not to mention the way his spicy cologne teased her nostrils and how each time his hand brushed hers, her heart skipped a beat. A curious thrumming filled her body and the type of thoughts running through her head had no business in a church.

She determinedly forced her attention back to the sermon, to the message of hope and promises fulfilled. Every so often she'd glance at Derek, but his eyes and attention were on the minister. On her other side Mickie hummed happily under her breath.

The day, which had started out so simply, had taken an odd turn. What worried Rachel the most was she didn't mind. Not one bit.

"Are you coming to brunch with us?" Lexi asked Derek after the service ended, taking the words right out of Rachel's mouth.

She'd planned to extend the invitation immediately after the benediction, but Nick had called out a welcome from farther down the pew and then David and July had hurried over. With everyone talking, Rachel could barely get a word in.

"The food at The Coffeepot is great." David cast a

pointed glance at Travis, who'd just sauntered up with Mary Karen and her three boys. "Though I can't vouch for the quality of the company."

"Hey." Travis punched David in the shoulder. "The Almighty has big ears."

Mary Karen grinned. "It's nothing He doesn't already know."

"I appreciate the invitation," Derek said. "But I ate before church specifically so I could head to the slopes to get some skiing in before the storm hits this afternoon."

Beside Rachel, the humming stopped.

"I wish I could go with you," Travis said. "But I've got a patient in labor and need to stay close."

"We're still on for Friday?" Derek asked.

"You bet," Travis said. "That's my day off and one of my partners is taking call."

After saying their goodbyes, the couples hurried off, children in tow. Rachel understood the hasty departure. The Coffeepot was *the* place to go after Sunday services and you had to get there right away to get a table.

From where she stood, Rachel rested her back against the pew, pretending her off-balanced feeling had to do with her new high heels and not the way Derek made her feel. "Are you going to Snow King or Jackson Hole?"

"I'm thinking Jackson Hole, though I may change my mind," Derek said, seemingly no longer in a rush to leave. "I'm not meeting anyone, so it's just where I feel like going once I leave the house."

"The conditions couldn't be better," Rachel said, unable to keep a hint of wistfulness from her tone. The mountain slopes already had a good solid base of snow and a recent storm had added eight inches of perfect powder.

Mickie stepped forward. "I want to learn to ski. Addie knows how and she's only eight."

By the time the little girl finished speaking her cheeks were bright red. Still, her eyes remained riveted on Derek's face.

Rachel clamped her hand gently but firmly on Mickie's shoulder. She knew the little girl wanted to learn to ski, but teaching her wasn't Derek's responsibility. "I'll take you this week, sweetie. I promise."

"If you don't have plans for the afternoon, we could all go together," Derek said.

"You don't have to invite us—"

"Sure he does," Mickie interrupted.

"No." Rachel shot her a warning glance. "He doesn't."

"I want you to come." Before Rachel knew what was happening he reached over and took her hand. "You. And Mickie."

His thumb caressed her palm, making rational thought difficult.

"Mickie doesn't have anything to wear—" she stammered.

"We can stop at one of the village stores," Derek said in a husky baritone that sent shivers up her spine.

"Please, Rachel. Pleeeeease." Mickie grabbed her sleeve. "I really want to go skiing with you and Mr. Rossi."

Over Mickie's curly brown head, Derek's eyes found hers.

"It's up to you." The liquid blue depths drew her in,

tempting her. Asking her to venture from the solid shore of what she'd always known to a place where she could be over her head in an instant. The moment the thought tried to take hold in her mind, she rejected it. What a ridiculous, fanciful thought.

"Please, Rachel," Mickie said.

"Please, Rachel," Derek echoed.

Rachel settled her gaze on Mickie. She was doing this for the child, she told herself. Not for any other reason. "It looks like you get your wish. Today you're going to learn to ski."

Mickie let out a whoop.

"Shh—" Rachel said, but her smile took any sting from the admonition.

"I'm glad you're coming," Derek said softly, his gaze widening to include Mickie.

"Thank you for inviting us," Mickie said.

"I don't think we gave him much choice," Rachel laughed.

"He wanted us to come with him, didn't you, Mr. Rossi?"

"I did." Derek shot the child a wink, though his gaze remained focused on Rachel. "After all, what man wouldn't like to spend the afternoon with two beautiful women?"

Chapter Seven

Rachel stood at the bottom of the bunny slope at Jackson Hole Mountain Resort and concluded that for someone who hadn't been around little girls much, Derek was doing a good job making Mickie happy. Right now the child stood at the crest of the small mound of snow, awkwardly positioning her skis, ready to give the downhill experience one more try.

They'd spent a good couple hours picking out clothes and equipment. Mickie had groaned when she'd insisted on a helmet, but Rachel hadn't budged.

Derek had wanted to be the one to teach Mickie to ski, but Rachel convinced him that it would be good for the little girl to be around other children. Thankfully when they'd dropped her off at ski school, the other children in her class had also been wearing helmets.

They'd hung around for a while and watched. Mickie hadn't been lying when she'd said she had zero experience on skis. In fact, she'd been the worst in her class. But her tenacity impressed them both and eventually she'd mastered the basic skills of stopping, turning and getting up from a fall.

While she and the other children were practicing, Derek and Rachel were able to get in some ski time of their own. It was an exhilarating experience. Rachel had always been much better than Tom, which meant that when they skied together it had to be on slopes that were too easy for her. She and Derek had headed straight for the expert slopes. She'd been having so much fun that she could have skied all afternoon. But all too soon they'd had to get back to Mickie.

"Watch me, Mr. Rossi," the child called out. "Rachel, watch me."

Once she was confident their eyes were on her, Mickie pushed off with her poles and skied down the small slope for the first time without falling.

"Woo-hoo," Derek yelled, giving her a big thumbs-up.

Rachel snapped another picture. Derek had grabbed a camera out of his glove box and presented it to her on their way to the village. She'd put it immediately to use, taking candid shots of Derek and Mickie in the Escalade. Then, when they'd stopped to shop for ski clothes and equipment, Rachel had taken pictures while the child shyly modeled the latest fashions. She and Derek had wanted to stay during the practice session and get a few photos, but Mickie had said it would make her too nervous.

"This was super fun," Mickie said when they met her at the bottom of the hill. "I want to come here again."

"Definitely," Derek said. Rachel could tell he was pleased by the child's enthusiasm. "In fact, you'll probably be sick of this place by the time January comes."

"Never." Mickie's eyes shone. "This was the best day of my life."

They waited while Mickie sat on a bench and removed her skis, then headed to the parking lot. On the way, another family joined them. Rachel recognized the daughter from Mickie's ski class and the two girls chattered happily all the way to Derek's vehicle.

After saying goodbye to her new friend and exchanging phone numbers, Mickie hopped inside the truck. Rachel waited outside with Derek while he stowed their gear. "I think we showed you today that girls can enjoy outdoor activities and sports as much as boys."

"Some girls," he said with a rueful smile. "Not all."

She wasn't sure who he was thinking of, but she understood. Tom had tolerated skiing but had never had the passion for it that she did. Impulsively, Rachel looped her arm through Derek's. "Well, the two with you today had a fabulous time."

His blue eyes met hers. "That's because you…and Mickie…are special."

Ignoring the little sparks of electricity from his nearness, Rachel laughed. "Don't tell me you just figured that out?"

By the time they were ready to leave the Teton Village area, the snow had began to fall again and darkness was rapidly descending. Thankfully, the blizzard that had been predicted hadn't yet materialized. The digital display on the vehicle's dash said it was suppertime.

Derek's growling stomach had already made that connection.

He slanted a sideways glance at Rachel and marveled at her wholesome good looks. The blue of her parka accentuated the color of her eyes. She'd pulled off her stocking cap on the drive from Teton Village, her golden hair a mass of curls brushing her shoulders. With a slight flush of pink on her cheeks, she looked like one of those angels that topped a Christmas tree. He thought about telling her so, but decided not only would that be corny but also inappropriate. After all, she was his friend, not his girlfriend.

Derek wheeled the Escalade out of the Teton Village parking area and onto Moose Wilson Road. "Anyone else but me hungry?"

"I am," Mickie said.

Rachel smiled at the child's enthusiasm. "Me, too."

"We should all stop somewhere and eat," Mickie said.

"That does sound like fun." Rachel turned in her seat to face Mickie. "But I'm afraid I didn't budget for eating out this evening. I'm sorry, kiddo."

In the rearview mirror, Derek could see the disappointment on the child's face. But she didn't beg. It was as if she knew most of the money Rachel had spent today had been on her.

The ski jacket and pants, helmet, even the cost of the lessons had all come out of Rachel's pocket. Derek had wanted to pay, but she'd politely but very firmly turned him down.

"But I'd be happy to make something for all of us," Rachel offered.

Which, Derek realized, would necessitate Rachel using her groceries to feed him.

"I have an even better idea," he said. "Why don't we go to my place and I'll fix dinner?"

"We couldn't impose—"

"I have an ulterior motive," he said.

"What's an all-terrier motive?" Mickie asked.

Derek didn't crack a smile. "It means that while you're there, I'd like you to help me decorate my tree."

Mickie's eyes drew together in thought. "Decorating a tree takes a lot of time, huh?"

"Are you saying that you don't want to do it?"

"No, I want to do it. I think it would be super-duper fun." Mickie's enthusiasm seemed to grow with each word. "Rachel doesn't put up her tree until Christmas Eve. By then it will be almost time for me to leave."

Two spots of color settled on Rachel's cheeks. "I explained that was always our tradition."

Derek knew exactly who "our" was. He wanted to ask her why she felt the need to hold so tightly on to past traditions, but kept his mouth shut. When she chose to put up her tree wasn't his business.

"What do you say, Rachel? Can we go to Mr. Rossi's house? Can we, please?"

Rachel shook her head. "Fred has been alone most of the day. I hate to leave him alone all evening as well. I'm afraid we're going to have to pass."

If it wasn't for the tears in Mickie's eyes, Derek wouldn't have pressed the issue. But he agreed with the child. Waiting until Christmas Eve to decorate a tree was way too long.

"We can pick up Fred and take him to my place.

There's no reason he can't come along." Derek's tone turned persuasive. "Please, give me this opportunity to return your hospitality."

"Yeah, Rachel," Mickie said. "Give him a chance to return your hos-bis-tality."

Rachel smiled. "Okay. We'd love to join you."

Something that sounded a lot like "Thank You, God" came from the backseat.

"Dinner won't be anything fancy," Derek said. "How does chili sound?"

"Sounds good to me," Rachel said.

"How 'bout it, Mick? Are you happy?"

In the backseat, Mickie grinned. "Very happy."

A peaceful calm settled over Derek's home. The chili had been polished off, the dishwasher loaded and the dog fed. That only left…the tree. The majestic sixteen-foot Douglas fir stood in front of the great room windows practically begging to be turned into a Christmas tree.

When Rachel bent over to pull another box of ornaments from the closet, Derek paused to admire the view. Blue jeans hugged her long, slender legs and caressed her firm backside. He let his gaze linger, wishing his body would keep its feelings to itself.

"I have to tell you something."

Derek shifted his gaze and found Mickie with Fred beside her. A tiny frown worried the child's brow. He crouched down until he was at eye level with her, fending off Fred's attempt to kiss him. "Tell me."

"I don't know the right way to decorate a tree." Her frown deepened. "I'm afraid I'll do it wrong."

For a second he wondered if she was joking. Then he saw the flicker of fear in her eyes. They'd told Mickie to share her feelings. Now that she had, Derek was determined to be respectful and not minimize them.

"Are you saying there's a correct way to decorate a tree?" He kept his tone deliberately conversational.

She nodded and chewed on her lip, her gaze focused on her feet.

As if picking up on her stress, Fred whined and nudged her hand with his nose. Mickie looped one arm around his neck and he quieted.

Derek waited, knowing she'd tell him more, when she was ready. It didn't take long.

"Uncle Wayne used to get angry if I didn't put the ornaments on the tree the way he wanted. But he wouldn't tell me what the right way was." Tears welled in the little girl's eyes. "I want to do it right. I don't want you or Rachel to be mad at me. Ever."

Out of the corner of his eye Derek saw Rachel straighten and turn.

He rested his hand on Mickie's shoulder. "In this house there is no right or wrong way. That goes for stringing the lights or hanging the ornaments. But I'm glad you let me know you were concerned."

"I think we should put the ornaments on first." Rachel placed a box filled with them at his feet.

"I've always put the lights on first," Derek said. "What do you say, Mick? Lights or ornaments? Remember, there's no right or wrong answer."

His last words were drowned out by the raucous tune "Ding Dong the Witch Is Dead" coming from

Rachel's phone. "I'm sorry," she said quickly, her cheeks reddening. "I should answer this."

Derek had assumed she'd talk there, but instead, she moved to the kitchen and out of earshot.

"Do you think something is wrong?" Mickie said. "Rachel looked worried. Don't you think she looked worried?"

"Maybe a little bit," Derek reluctantly conceded, relieved when Rachel returned to the room.

"Everything okay?" he asked.

Rachel let her gaze linger on the banister decorated with tiny homemade wreaths made of evergreen tied together with a ribbon garland, not sure what to say. She'd been determined not to bring up Tom tonight. But there was no way around it now. "It was my in-laws' annual Christmas call."

"You're still in touch with them." Derek spoke in a matter-of-fact tone, the words more of a statement than a question.

Rachel felt compelled to defend their action, though she didn't understand it herself. "They *are* Tom's parents."

"Hey, I didn't mean anything." He lifted his hands, an ornament in each one. "It's…nice…that they keep in touch."

"I think it's weird," Mickie said.

Rachel inhaled sharply, too stunned to reply.

"Mickie." A hint of reproach filled Derek's voice. "You owe Rachel an apology."

Instead, Mickie's chin lifted in a stubborn tilt. "But why would his mom and dad call her? *Why?*"

Attitude dripped from the last word and out of the

corner of Rachel's eye she saw Derek's expression darken.

"We had some business to discuss," Rachel said.

"Even if you didn't, you were a part of their family for a good number of years," Derek said. "I'm sure you had a close relationship during that time. It's only natural they'd want to keep in touch."

Mickie rolled her eyes.

"Honey." Rachel stepped close and placed a gentle hand on the child's shoulder. While she didn't want to ruin the afternoon, she couldn't let such behavior go unchallenged. "Rolling your eyes is rude. I'd appreciate it if you didn't do that again."

Mickie's bottom lip trembled. "I'm sorry."

Motherly love rose up inside Rachel. She wrapped her arms around the girl, pulling her close, planting a kiss on the top of Mickie's curly head. "Forgiven."

Rachel lifted her head and her eyes met Derek's. His slow smile of approval sent warmth coursing all the way to the tips of her toes.

She pulled her gaze away, her heart full, but at the same time, light. "Why are we standing around? We've got a tree to decorate."

"It's bee-u-ti-ful." Mickie clasped her hands together and stared at the large tree, her eyes as bright as the lights gracing its branches.

"We did good," Derek agreed.

Instead of a tedious task, hanging the ornaments and stringing the lights had been a joyous endeavor, thanks mostly to Rachel. She'd made it, well, fun. Before they started, she'd insisted he look through his friend's vast

CD collection for some Christmas music. Surprisingly, they'd found not only traditional holiday classics but some children's tunes as well. Right now a tune from "A Chipmunk Christmas" blared from the Bose speakers.

Rachel stood beside him, gazing at the tree. The glow on her face matched the wonder on the child's face in front of her. Derek fought an almost-uncontrollable urge to slip his arm around her shoulder. Only the knowledge that such an action could ruin the moment kept his hands at his side.

"Look." Mickie pointed to the large floor-to-ceiling window almost obscured by the large tree. "It's still snowing."

Rachel's eyes widened. "Ohmigod."

Derek moved past her to the glass. The thick blanket of white covering the ground had grown significantly since they'd gotten home. The way the flakes were falling, the snow was destined to get even deeper.

"I can't believe I didn't notice it was getting so bad." Rachel's fingers curved around his arm as she leaned close for a better look.

Derek inhaled the clean fresh scent of her. The dulcet sounds of Kenny G's sax had replaced the raucous Chipmunk music and the candles they'd lit earlier added a warm intimacy. For several heartbeats he stood, reveling in the moment which seemed suspended in time.

Until Mickie wiggled between them. "Are we snowed in?"

The child couldn't have sounded happier if Santa Claus laden with gifts had dropped from the chimney.

"I'm sure we can make it home." Though the words

were confident, Rachel's voice wavered and concern filled her blue eyes.

A blast of wind hit the windows. The house shuddered.

Derek shook his head. "It's not worth the risk."

"We don't want to get in an accident," Mickie said.

Hiding a smile, Derek glanced at Fred asleep on the floor in front of the fireplace. It was as if the dog had already settled in for the night.

"I'm afraid you don't have a choice." Derek turned and met Rachel's gaze. "You're going to have to spend the night."

"With you?" Rachel's voice came out on a high-pitched squeak.

When Derek grinned, it made her feel even more foolish.

"Well, I don't think my bed is big enough for the four of us," he said, and she swore she saw a twinkle in his eyes. "But there are three extra bedrooms, so I'm sure you'll be comfortable."

Although his expression gave nothing away and he was being a perfect gentleman about the situation, the electricity crackling in the air told her if Mickie wasn't present, his answer may have been different.

Still, Rachel hesitated. What would Mickie's case worker think if she found out they'd spent the night with a single man? Especially one as handsome and charismatic as Derek Rossi.

"You can't put Mickie—and yourself—at risk," he said softly, as if he'd read her thoughts. "The only sensible thing is to stay."

"My uncle Wayne went into a ditch once when it

was snowing," Mickie piped up from in front of the fire where she now sat, scratching Fred's neck. "I was in the backseat. I hurt my head."

"Oh, my," Rachel said.

"It wasn't even snowing as hard as it is now," Mickie continued. "But Uncle Wayne had been smoking those stinky little cigarettes, the ones that made his eyes all red. I don't think he could see very well."

Derek stiffened and muttered something Rachel couldn't make out.

"You've convinced me." Rachel prayed she was making the right decision. "We'll stay."

"Yippee." Mickie scrambled to her feet and Fred lurched to a standing position beside her. "I want to see my room."

"Derek can show it to us later," Rachel said. "Closer to bedtime."

"But I'm tired now," Mickie protested. "Fred and I want to go to bed."

Rachel tilted her head, confused. "Now? It's only nine."

Even though only moments before she'd looked wide awake, Mickie yawned loudly and flung her arms out in a big stretch.

"I can't help it that I'm tired," she said.

"You have had a big day." Rachel slanted an apologetic smile in Derek's direction. "I guess we'll go to bed now."

"No. No. No." Mickie practically shouted the words. "You stay up and…talk…to Mr. Rossi. I'm not a baby. I can go to bed by myself."

The child's generosity touched Rachel's heart. "But you'll be in a strange bedroom."

"I've slept in a lot of strange bedrooms. Besides—" Mickie slipped her arm around the bloodhound's neck "—I have Fred."

"If you're sure…" Rachel said, still not convinced.

"I'm positive." Mickie's lips curved into a smile. "Absolutely positively positive."

Chapter Eight

"She's never gone to bed so easily." Rachel sank into the overstuffed leather love seat facing the stone fireplace.

A rustic end table separated her sofa from Derek's chair. While she was getting Mickie ready for bed, Derek had added more wood to the fire and brought out a bottle of wine.

He leaned forward and handed her a glass. "This is the perfect way to end a wonderful day."

Soft piano music played in the background. The light from the candles cast interesting shadows across his face. Rachel could see why he always had a beautiful woman on his arm. Not only was he intelligent and an all-around good guy, but he was also super sexy.

She pulled her gaze from him and took a sip of wine. The full-bodied red was smooth against her tongue.

She let the delicious taste linger for a moment before swallowing. "This is fabulous."

Derek's lips quirked upward. "It's a very good year."

"If I didn't know better, I'd think you were trying to seduce me," Rachel said, waving her glass in the air.

"If Mickie weren't here, you'd probably be right." His eyes glittered in the dim light and the sexy intent in his gaze thrilled her.

Rachel laughed. "Promises. Promises."

Some might accuse her of playing with fire, but Rachel knew she was in no danger of getting burned. This casual flirting was just that, flirting. And as close as she planned to get to the flame.

As she'd expected, Derek simply smiled. He leaned back, holding the stem of the wineglass loosely between his fingers. "Tell me about your husband."

The fire that had been flickering quite nicely in Rachel's belly was quashed by a splash of cold water. "Why?"

"I'm curious." Derek lifted the glass to his lips and took a sip. "Unless it's hard for you to speak of him."

"Not at all." Although it *was* awkward to discuss her husband with the first man who'd inspired salacious thoughts since Tom had passed away.

"Tom," she said, savoring the feel of the name against her tongue, "was a geologist. He worked for the U.S. Geologic Survey."

"That tells me what he did," Derek said, his gaze hooded. "Not what he was like."

It was a valid point. Tom's career as a geologist hadn't

defined him any more than Derek's pro-ball career defined him.

"I called him my 'gentle giant.'" Rachel's laugh caught in her throat. "He was a big man, six-four with broad shoulders and a full beard."

"You thought he was the most handsome man in the world." It was a statement, not a question.

Rachel widened her eyes. "How did you know?"

"I can hear it in your voice."

"Strangers were often intimidated because of his size and because he didn't have much to say." She'd found it odd that people were always quick to point out her husband's reticence—as if it was a negative—when it was that same quiet strength that had drawn her to him after her parents died. "He was a kind, sweet man and I loved him with my whole heart."

"Sounds like a great guy." Derek took a sip of wine. "Did you grow up together around here?"

Rachel swirled the wine in her glass. "Actually, we both grew up in Wisconsin. We met in college, married after graduation, then moved here. Tom loved Wyoming. Called the state a 'geologist's paradise.'"

The comment earned her a quick smile. "Was it hard to leave your family?"

Family. Her heart twisted. She didn't have a family. Not anymore.

"My parents died in a car accident my freshman year in college. Tom was close to his family." Rachel glanced down at her hands. "When we married I'd hoped I could be close to them, too."

Derek sat his glass down and steepled his fingers beneath his chin, giving her his full attention. "Something tells me that didn't happen."

"Given more time, it might have," Rachel said, wanting to be fair. "But we got off to a rocky start. They thought Tom should wait a few more years before marrying. And they were completely opposed to him leaving Wisconsin. He assured them that moving here was his idea—which was the truth—but his mom and dad blamed me."

"Nice."

"It was what it was." Rachel shrugged. "Tom and I had a good marriage. A happy one." She paused and her lips quirked up in a smile. "Made even happier by the fact that there was thirteen hundred miles between us and his family."

Derek chuckled, then sobered. "Yet they still call you."

"Once a year." She tightened her fingers around the stem of her glass. "The first year they called me on the day he died. I put a stop to that."

"Too hard?"

"Yes, of course," Rachel said with a sigh. "But more than that, there were so many good things about Tom to remember...why focus on that last horrible day?"

"If you don't mind my asking, what happened to him?"

Rachel studied the flickering flames. It was amazing how a life could burn so brightly one minute, then in an instant be snuffed out.

"It happened three years ago." She leaned back and closed her eyes for a second. "Christmas was five days away. We were so excited. This would be the last Christmas we'd celebrate, just the two of us."

Derek's head cocked to one side.

"I was pregnant." Her voice quivered slightly. "Twenty-two weeks."

Even though he covered it well, she could see the surprise in his eyes. "What happened?"

The question appeared wrung from his lips.

"We both had the day off work. We slept late since we'd been out caroling with some friends from church the night before." Rachel gazed into the dark liquid in her glass and familiar fingers of guilt wrapped around her heart. "Instead of going out, we decided to eat at home that morning. But I was craving orange juice. While I made breakfast, Tom made a juice run to the convenience store not far from our apartment."

While the story never came easily, this time she found herself choking on the words. Maybe because she'd just spoken with Tom's parents. Perhaps because in only eight days it would be the twentieth of December.

Derek didn't press her for more details. Instead, he sipped his wine and waited. Even in the dim light she could see the sympathy in his eyes.

Rachel cleared her throat. "While Tom was at the store a man came in and demanded money from the female clerk. The clerk resisted and when the robber hit her in the face with his gun, Tom intervened and was shot. He died on the floor with the carton of orange juice still in his hand."

"That must have been horrible for you." Derek placed his glass on the table, his eyes never leaving hers.

"The sheriff came to the door." Rachel pulled her

gaze from his and focused on a spot over his left shoulder. "All I could think of was that breakfast was almost ready. How silly was that?"

"Not silly at all." His words were soft as a caress. "You were in shock."

"I did my best to hold it together," Rachel said. "I always thought I was a strong person, but I felt so lost. So alone. Tom had been my anchor and suddenly he was gone. There was just me…and the baby. Our poor sweet baby."

Her voice broke and a few more tears slid down her cheek.

Without a word, Derek rose, then dropped to her side, his arm slipping around her shoulders. She told herself to push him away. Instead, she leaned her head against his shoulder.

"The baby came early. There were complications," she whispered, although there was no one around except the two of them. "I almost died. When they told me our son hadn't made it, I wished I had died."

"I'm glad you didn't." Derek leaned his head against hers, his voice soft as a whisper against her cheek.

"It was just so hard…" Rachel said with a sigh.

"I wish I could have been there for you," he said, his blue eyes dark as midnight.

For a long moment neither of them spoke.

Although she hadn't known Derek long, Rachel trusted him. She rested her head on his shoulder and let herself draw comfort from his strength.

Rachel wasn't sure if it was the wine or the warmth from his body. All she knew was her lids were suddenly too heavy to keep open. She closed her eyes…only for a second.

* * *

Mickie waited until almost midnight before creeping down the stairs, her heart pounding like a great big drum. If there was any kissing going on, she needed to see it. Kissing would confirm they were making progress.

She told herself she wasn't spying. She simply wanted to make sure Mr. Rossi and Rachel were…getting along okay.

At first she couldn't find them. It was Fred who finally located them curled up together on the sofa in front of the fireplace. Rachel's head was pressed against his chest. Mr. Rossi's arms were tightly wrapped around her.

Mickie's heart pounded so loudly that she worried the sound might wake them. She was still standing in the shadows, trying not to breathe, when she heard Mr. Rossi murmur something in his sleep and kiss Rachel's hair. When Rachel smiled and snuggled even more tightly against him, Mickie let out the breath she'd been holding.

This was even better than she'd dared hope. Not only had Mr. Rossi kissed Rachel, but she was also napping with him. Mickie couldn't wait to tell Addie.

After Rachel and Mickie left, Derek spent the rest of the day working out and watching baseball films. But even though his calendar was clear, he had the feeling that he was forgetting something. It wasn't until almost eight that he realized that *something* was his mother's birthday.

Although in California most people would consider

8:00 p.m. to be early, his mom wasn't in California. She was vacationing in Florida where it was 10:00 p.m. If Derek was going to call, he needed to do it now. Or risk taking the chance of catching her after she'd gone to bed…with Jim?

Derek shoved the disturbing image aside before it could take hold and become imprinted on his brain. He didn't know—didn't want to know—if his mother was intimate with her longtime man-friend. In terms of his mother's romantic activities, Don't Ask, Don't Tell was his motto.

Grabbing the cocoa he'd just made for himself, Derek took it and his phone into the living room. This way, while he offered his mother birthday wishes, he could admire the tree.

He paused in the doorway, taking in the white lights, the colorful ornaments and the elaborate silver star at the top of the tree.

Although it was designer beautiful, Derek found himself thinking of his childhood trees. He didn't need to close his eyes to remember the spindly pines decorated with items he and his sister had made in school…and the special ornaments his mother gave them every year. He wished he'd thought to get Mickie some sort of ornament to mark this year, her first Christmas with Rachel. Her *last* Christmas with Rachel.

A wave of sadness washed over him. Mickie deserved a family. She deserved a mom and dad who would give her not only love, but also stability. She deserved a dog like Fred. Derek wished he could adopt the little girl, but his hours were crazy. No, Mickie deserved more than he could give her at this point in his life.

With the cup firmly in his grasp, Derek crossed the room and plopped down on the sofa where he'd slept last night. Correction. Where he *and* Rachel had slept last night.

He smiled, remembering the look on her face when she'd opened her eyes to find herself snuggled up against his chest. Her cheeks had turned bright red, the desire in her eyes overpowered by regret. So, instead of kissing her, he'd made a joke. And then he'd thrown together a quick breakfast for the three of them.

He hoped she'd relax, but the beautiful blonde's shoulders remained stiff all through breakfast. In fact, she'd kept her eyes fixed on the door as if looking for an opportunity to bolt. Talk about an ego crusher.

Derek hadn't been surprised when right after they'd finished eating, she'd announced it was time for her to get home. Even Mickie whining that she really, really, *really* wanted to stay longer hadn't dissuaded her. Worse yet, she'd made it clear she never wanted to see him again.

Derek took a sip of hot chocolate, flinching at the scalding sensation against his tongue. Rachel wasn't an easy one to figure out. He'd never known a woman who ran so hot, then so cold. Exhaling a breath that sounded suspiciously like a sigh, Derek hit speed dial.

A familiar feminine voice—thankfully sounding completely awake—answered on the second ring.

"Happy birthday, Mom."

"Derek, honey. What perfect timing." The lilt in her voice made him smile. He remembered all too well the years immediately following his father's death when all the joy seemed to have been sucked out of her. "I just got off the phone with your sister."

"Everything okay with her?"

"Sarah's good," his mother said. "She asked if I'd heard from you, wondered how you were getting along."

"I'll give her a call when I hang up." Derek relaxed against the back of the sofa. "But right now I want to know how your day has been."

"Fabulous," Leigh Rossi said with a throaty chuckle. "Jim spoiled and pampered me all day. Tonight he took me to a restaurant overlooking the ocean for dinner. Wine. Candlelight. Very romantic."

Romantic. Dangerous territory when it came to his mother.

"Sounds…great."

"Now tell me all about Derek. Are you happy with your decision to spend Christmas in Jackson Hole? Have you gotten in any skiing?"

"No regrets at all." Derek went on to tell her about the Tetons, the steep slopes and the great skiing which led to him mentioning Travis, Rachel and Mickie. And who could talk about December in Wyoming without bringing in the weather? "Rachel and Mickie came over last night to help me decorate my Christmas tree. By the time we stuck the star on top, the snow was falling so heavily they ended up having to spend the night."

"Oh, Derek." His mother exhaled a heavy sigh. "I really don't think that was a good idea."

Derek immediately understood his mother's concern, but he also knew he hadn't given her the whole story. "I agree there was an impressionable child to consider, but the roads were impassable. Besides we each had our own bedroom."

"That wasn't my worry. I know you would never be inappropriate around a child."

Derek took a sip of hot cocoa and waited for her to continue. For several seconds all he heard was the beating of his own heart. "So what's the problem?"

"You told me you were spending this time in Jackson Hole to figure out why you keep falling in love with the wrong women." Her tone was suddenly schoolteacher firm, the voice of the mother from his childhood. "And what happened to your six-month moratorium on dating?"

Even though Derek sat quite comfortably on the overstuffed leather sofa, he felt as if his back had just been shoved against the wall. He resisted the urge to lash out. To shout that how he lived his life was none of her business. But he remained silent. And in control of his temper.

This was her birthday. She was his mother. Of course she was concerned. And in his heart, he knew she only wanted the best for him. However, that didn't mean he was going to let her rebuke him like one of her former students.

"We both know I had good reasons for ending those engagements." Derek placed his cup on the end table and stood, moving to the window to stare unseeing at the snow-covered trees. "There was no way I could have predicted that Jenna would refuse to leave Minnesota when the Angels drafted me."

"You dated your entire senior year of college," his mother pointed out. "I still can't believe you'd never talked about what would happen if you got a good draft offer."

Actually, he'd talked a lot about his draft hopes. Jenna had never said a peep about not wanting to move. Only later did she confide she'd assumed he wouldn't get drafted. While he'd been dreaming of a life in the major leagues, she'd been planning on making a home in Edina, close to her parents.

She hadn't been willing to make any concessions.

But then, neither had he.

"We were too young," he said. Then, because that sounded like a cop-out, he added, "*I* was too young."

"That excuse doesn't work for you and Heather," his mom not-so-gently reminded him. "Twenty-five was old enough to know better."

Losing Heather had hurt. When he'd first met her she'd just broken up with her longtime boyfriend. Still, the knowledge that she was on the rebound hadn't stopped Derek from falling hard and fast.

Three months after their first date he'd asked her to become his wife. She'd happily agreed. The wedding announcements had already been mailed when Heather had come to him and confessed she wasn't in love with him. They'd called off the wedding and she'd married her ex-boyfriend six months later.

At the time the news had sent him reeling.

"I loved Heather," Derek said, amazed that the loss no longer hurt as it once did. "The problem was, she didn't love me."

"You rushed into that relationship," his mother pointed out.

"I didn't do that with Niki," he said. "We'd been

dating over a year and I was in no hurry to nail things down. I only asked her to marry me because she told me she was pregnant. What was I supposed to do when I discovered she'd made it up? Marry her anyway?"

His voice had a bite to it but doggonit, if anyone should understand, it should be his own mother.

"Honey, I know your heart was in the right place." Her tone gentled. "What worries me now is the affection I already hear in your voice for this woman and the child."

"You don't need to worry. I can take care of myself."

"I don't doubt that. But you're a romantic. You've always wanted a wife and family. This woman and child may seem to be what you've been looking—"

"Mom," Derek interrupted, knowing this was one lecture she didn't need to give. "Let me put this another way. You don't need to worry because nothing is going to happen between Rachel and me."

"How can you be so sure?" Even from two thousand miles away, her skepticism came through loud and clear.

"Because Rachel made it perfectly clear she doesn't want to see me again."

Chapter Nine

Derek rounded the corner of a grocery store aisle and pulled his cart to a dead stop. At the far end of the long aisle, Rachel and Mickie stood, intently focused on the shelves in front of them. For a split second, he was tempted to back up and immediately head to the checkout. But he rejected the impulse. He wasn't a coward. Besides, it was good to see Rachel, to see them both.

He wheeled his cart purposefully down the aisle. When he was about five feet away, Mickie turned in his direction.

She shrieked his name and ran to him, slamming into him with a force that would have done an NFL tackle proud. "I've missed you so much."

"I've missed you, too." Until this moment he hadn't quite realized how much. Derek awkwardly patted the top of her curly head, then put his hands on her shoulders and held her at arm's length. "Let me look at you."

Although the child was dressed as usual in jeans and a long-sleeved cotton shirt, she seemed different than the first time he'd seen her. Spending time with Rachel had been good for her. She appeared happy, not worried or stressed. She looked, he decided, like a typical ten-year-old grocery shopping with her mom.

Conscious of Rachel's eyes on him, Derek kept his attention focused on Mickie a few seconds longer. "I swear you've grown six inches since I last saw you."

Mickie giggled, the sound echoing in the large, mostly empty store. "You just saw me two days ago."

Had it really been only forty-eight hours?

"We're picking out stuff to make tacos tonight," Mickie said. "Do you like tacos? Maybe you could—"

"Mickie. Stop." Rachel's tone was soft but firm. She shifted her gaze. When those blue eyes met his, a jolt of awareness shot through him.

"Hello, Rachel." He let his gaze linger. She wore the parka he liked, the one that made her eyes look the color of the sky. Her hair was pulled back into a low ponytail and, unless he was mistaken, she didn't appear to be wearing any makeup. She'd never been more lovely.

"Hi, Derek. What brings you to Super Saver at this hour of the morning?" Her polite tone was one usually reserved for strangers or very casual acquaintances.

"Empty refrigerator." He chuckled, trying to defuse the tension. The death grip she had on a package of flour tortillas told him she felt uncomfortable. There was no reason for her to feel that way. Derek understood that she was still hung up on her dead husband and worried he wanted more than she could give. The funny thing was he wasn't looking for a relationship with her. Or anyone.

But he *would* like to be her friend. He briefly considered telling her just that, but Mickie stood there listening intently to every word, just like she had the other morning.

"Hey, Mr. All-Star."

Derek turned and Ron walked up, carrying a carton of orange juice in one hand and a package of bacon in the other.

"Didn't expect to see anyone I knew this morning." The older man widened his smile to include Rachel and Mickie. "You three together?"

"Actually, I'm shocked to see both of you here." Rachel brushed a strand of hair back from her face with a self-conscious gesture. "Teaches me to leave home without makeup."

"I think you look beautiful," Ron said gallantly. "Doesn't she, Derek?"

"Very nice." Derek knew that was an understatement, but the way things were between them, less seemed more appropriate.

Rachel ducked her head for a second and her cheeks darkened to a becoming dusky rose color. Then she lifted her gaze. "Well, on that high note, Mickie and I are headed to the checkout."

Mickie made a sound of protest.

Derek gave her a wink. "See you around, kid."

"Really?" Mickie's eyes lit up.

"Jackson Hole isn't that big," Derek said. "I have no doubt our paths will cross again."

When he caught the expression in the child's eyes,

he vowed that if he didn't run into her again by the time he was ready to leave town, he'd look her up just to say goodbye.

"I'll make sure of it," he said. Just because Rachel didn't want to see him didn't mean he would desert Mickie.

Derek watched Rachel and Mickie take their cart and head to the cash registers at the front of the store, a knot in the pit of his stomach.

"I didn't mean to make 'em rush off." Ron frowned. "Especially since you're the first man Rachel has taken a shine to since her husband died."

"She doesn't like me," Derek said, shocked at the disappointed tone in his voice. "At least not in that way. You saw her. She couldn't wait to get away."

A hint of bitterness underscored his words. Okay, so maybe her going cold on him had hurt. A little.

"Son." Ron chuckled and shook his head. "I've been around a long time. I saw the look in her eyes. She's definitely interested, but something's got her spooked."

"Yeah, right," Derek scoffed.

Rachel afraid? She was the strongest woman he knew.

"Mark my word. One of these days she's going to get up the nerve to overcome whatever is holding her back. That's when she'll reach out to you." Under the fluorescent lights, Ron's eyes were dark, his expression completely serious. "And when she reaches out, if you care at all, don't hesitate. Because you may not get another chance."

The rustic ski lodge had been decorated for the holidays with wreaths and trees blazing with lights. But the festive scene didn't lift Mickie's spirits. Neither did the macaroni and cheese on her plate.

After a morning of tossing snowballs at Addie and falling down on the ski slopes, Mickie should have looked forward to lunch. But she wasn't hungry. Not even for her favorite meal.

She couldn't stop thinking about Mr. Rossi. She'd been so happy to see him at Super Saver. He'd seemed happy to see her, too. Then Rachel had ruined everything. Barbie would have never been so mean to Ken. That was why Barbie and Ken were together. And Rachel and Mr. Rossi were...not.

All morning Mickie had hidden her sadness from Rachel. When Addie had asked if she and Mickie could eat together by the giant fireplace, Mickie could have cheered. With Addie she didn't have to pretend she wasn't angry and so very sad.

Fortunately Rachel had run into a girlfriend from the hospital who'd accepted her invitation to lunch.

"Rachel barely talked to Mr. Rossi." Mickie pushed the cheesy noodles around on her plate, fighting back tears.

Although Addie appeared to be listening, she didn't immediately respond. Instead, she took a bite out of her humongous cheeseburger and chewed and chewed.

"I think he felt funny," Mickie said when Addie finally swallowed.

Addie's head cocked. "Funny?"

Mickie glanced at the table by the window where Rachel sat talking to her friend. "Before we left Mr. Rossi's house Monday morning I heard Rachel tell him she thought it 'best' if they didn't see each other again."

"Grown-ups do crazy things." Addie dipped a french fry into a cup of ketchup. "But Rachel likes Mr. Rossi. You said so yourself."

Mickie twisted her lips. "I thought she did. But you should have seen her at the grocery store this morning. She barely talked to him."

"Things will be better tomorrow."

Mickie stopped smashing the macaroni with her fork and met Addie's gaze. "How can you say that? You don't know."

"I know that everyone is getting together at Mrs. Vaughn's house to make Christmas candy." Addie shoved a fry dripping with ketchup into her mouth. "There's always lots of talking at those things. Trust me, they'll tell her she's crazy to not be with a nice guy like Mr. Rossi."

Mickie's heart skipped a beat. "Are you sure?"

"Positive."

The lump in Mickie's throat began to dissolve. "What if they don't convince her?"

"Then we'll figure something out. Failure—" Addie leaned across the table as if her plate of burger and fries weren't there "—isn't an option."

Mickie liked the sound of that and she liked the confidence in her friend's voice. For the first time in days, she let out the breath she'd been holding.

Addie was right. If Rachel's friends couldn't convince her she was acting silly, well, Mickie would come up with another plan.

Because, like Addie said, failure wasn't an option.

* * *

The afternoon at Mary Karen's house flew by. Rachel made peanut butter clusters, haystacks and divinity. After that she helped Mary Karen form Oreo balls. Keeping busy kept her mind off Derek. She'd been having great fun until she spoke without thinking.

When Lexi and July turned from the pan of fudge on Mary Karen's stove top with identical expressions of shock, Rachel knew she had some explaining to do.

It didn't take a rocket scientist to realize that when Mary Karen had asked how the skiing with Derek had gone on Sunday, Rachel should have simply said fine. Okay, maybe she'd have had to spill a few more details to keep her friends satisfied. Still, there'd been no reason to confess she'd spent an entire night in Derek Rossi's arms. No reason except Rachel desperately needed help sorting through her tangled emotions. And these women, her dearest friends, were as close to family as it got.

"Thank goodness the fudge is ready to pour." Lexi removed the pan from the stove. "I don't want to be distracted while you're telling us about your night of passion."

"I want to hear, too." July pulled a baby bottle from a pan of warm water where she'd been holding it submerged. "Just give me a second to get Adam situated."

July retrieved her nine-month-old son from the high chair where he'd been playing with a colorful ring of plastic keys and settled into a chair at the table. After testing the temperature of the formula against her wrist, she popped the nipple into his mouth.

Adam rested his head against his mother's chest,

sucking contentedly, his chubby fingers curling and uncurling.

Rachel's heart gave a ping. She'd once dreamed of holding Tom's baby the way July held Adam. But that was a lifetime ago. And her son, if he'd survived, would be closer to the age of Mary Karen's youngest, who sat on the floor crashing two trucks together.

"Okay, I'm ready now." July's green eyes snapped with curiosity. "Details, girl. Give us details."

Mary Karen leaned forward, resting her forearms on the table, her entire attention focused on Rachel. "How was he? Was the sex a grand slam?" She giggled at her own joke.

"Mickie and I were at Derek's house decorating his tree when that big storm moved in Sunday night." Had it really been only three days ago? "When we realized the roads would be impassable, he insisted we stay."

"Fast forward to the juicy part." Impatience underscored Mary Karen's words.

"And what juicy part would that be?" Rachel asked, discovering playing dumb could be, well, fun.

"The part where you got naked," Lexi called out from the stove where she stood pouring the melted chocolate into a baking dish.

"Lexi," Mary Karen hissed, gesturing with her head to almost three-year-old Logan. "Little ears."

Rachel hid a smile. "Are you telling me to keep it G-rated?"

July's lips formed a pout. "What fun is that?"

"If you could just avoid certain…words…in the telling I'd appreciate it." Mary Karen glanced at her youngest son. "Otherwise I'll hear them for weeks to come."

"Just give us the basics," Lexi said. "We'll fill in the blanks."

"Actually nothing happened," Rachel said.

"Uh, sorry." July shook her head. "Not buying it."

"It's the truth." Rachel wondered why she suddenly felt so regretful. "Derek was sitting next to me on the love seat. We were talking and drinking wine. I must have fallen asleep. When I woke up, he was right there."

"And then...?" July prompted.

"We got up and had breakfast." Rachel saw no reason to mention that she'd wanted him to kiss her. And, God help her, make love to her.

The intensity of her physical desire had shocked her. Although Mickie had been in no hurry to leave, she'd had to get out of there before Derek saw through her.

"Having a man in your life can be a beautiful thing," Lexi said, her eyes dreamy.

"If it's the right man," Mary Karen said.

"I *had* the right man," Rachel said, reminding her friends and herself. "I'm not looking for another."

"We're not saying you should marry the guy." July pulled the bottle from her son's mouth and gently lifted him to her shoulder.

"But you do enjoy his company," Mary Karen pointed out.

"And he's wonderful with Mickie," Lexi added.

"She adores him," Rachel admitted. "But I can't be with him because of her."

Lexi covered Rachel's hand with her own. "Since Tom died, your feet have been planted in the past. Why don't you try living in the present for a couple weeks?

No worries about yesterday. Or tomorrow. Simply enjoy the right now."

"You wouldn't be betraying Tom by having a male friend," Mary Karen said, her blue eyes dark and intense.

July offered a reassuring smile. "Nothing will happen that you don't want to happen."

They weren't saying anything Rachel hadn't told herself. Still, hearing the words from women she trusted made her feel better. Especially Mary Karen's comment.

Seeing Derek at the grocery store had been brutal. She hadn't known what to say without giving her secret yearnings away...so she'd said as little as possible.

"There's no reason we can't be friends," she said almost to herself. "I'll just have to make sure he understands there will be no kissing...or...anything else."

July tilted her head. "Has he tried to kiss you again?"

Rachel shook her head. Derek had been a perfect gentleman. It troubled her that the thought was more depressing than comforting.

"Well, when he makes a move, you can decide what you want to do," Lexi said. "After all, lots of friends kiss. Some even hop into bed with each other every now and then."

"Isn't that right, Mary Karen?" July's gaze settled on her sister-in-law. "You and Travis kiss sometimes, yet you're just friends."

Rachel turned to the young mother of three, not bothering to hide her surprise.

"There's absolutely nothing wrong with a little

friendly kissing," Mary Karen said in a cavalier tone, even though two bright spots of pink dotted her cheeks. "Where it can get hinky is when you let it go farther."

Chapter Ten

Mickie eased back into the shadows of the hall and gave Addie a silent high-five. But by the time she and her friend reached the living room, her joy had begun to sputter.

Over the years, Mickie had experienced her share of disappointments. Just because Rachel was agreeable to being friends with Derek at this moment didn't mean she'd be agreeable tomorrow. After all, look how she'd been to him at the store.

"The boys are fighting again," Addie sniffed.

Mickie pulled her thoughts back to the present, just in time to see Caleb grab a cell phone from his brother's hands, then leap from the sofa, his twin on his heels.

"Give it to me," Connor growled, holding out his hand.

"No," Caleb shouted, hiding the cell phone behind his back.

FREE Merchandise is 'in the Cards' for you!

Dear Reader,

We're giving away FREE MERCHANDISE!

Seriously, we'd like to reward you for reading this novel by giving you **FREE MERCHANDISE** worth over **$20**. And no purchase is necessary!

You see the Jack of Hearts sticker above? Paste that sticker in the box on the Free Merchandise Voucher inside. Return the Voucher promptly...and we'll send you valuable Free Merchandise!

Thanks again for reading one of our novels—and enjoy your Free Merchandise with our compliments!

Pam Powers

Pam Powers

P.S. Look inside to see what Free Merchandise is **"in the cards"** for you!

YOUR FREE MERCHANDISE INCLUDES...

2 FREE Silhouette Special Edition® Books

AND 2 FREE Mystery Gifts

FREE MERCHANDISE VOUCHER

2 FREE BOOKS
and
2 FREE GIFTS

Please send my Free Merchandise, consisting of
2 Free Books and **2 Free Mystery Gifts**.
I understand that I am under no obligation to buy
anything, as explained on the back of this card.

*About how many NEW paperback fiction books
have you purchased in the past 3 months?*

❑ 0-2   ❑ 3-6   ❑ 7 or more
E9EY   E9FC   E9FN

235/335 SDL

Please Print

FIRST NAME

LAST NAME

ADDRESS

APT.#   CITY

STATE/PROV.   ZIP/POSTAL CODE

▲ Detach card and mail today. No stamp needed. ▼

(SSE-12/10)

NO PURCHASE NECESSARY!

Mickie sighed. If this didn't get settled, she wouldn't be able to hear the television, much less talk to Addie about Rachel and Mr. Rossi. She stepped in front of Caleb. "Why won't you give Connor the phone?"

"Cuz he wants to text Travis and ask him if he'll take us to the movies Friday night." Caleb settled his gaze on his brother. "Stupid dodo head."

Mickie stared. The boy's eyes sparkled. It was almost as if Caleb *enjoyed* calling his brother names.

"You're the stupid one." Connor glared at his twin. "Everybody texts."

"Yeah, but they can spell," Caleb retorted.

Mickie glanced at Addie for interpretation of little-boy-speak.

"They're in kindergarten," Addie said in a stage whisper loud enough to reach any back row. "They don't know how to spell big words, like *movies*."

"That's why I said we should *call* Travis," Caleb said.

Mickie turned to Connor. "Forget texting until you're in first grade."

Connor expelled a harsh breath. "Fine," he said through clenched teeth. "Speed dial six."

The boys, along with their mother's phone, disappeared down the hall.

Rachel expelled a heavy sigh and sank into the soft sofa.

"What's the matter with you? You should be twirling right now." Addie flung out her arms and gave a little spin. "Didn't you hear? Your mom agreed to be Mr. Rossi's friend."

Her mom. Although Rachel wasn't her mother—not

yet anyway—Mickie liked the sound of the words. She held the hope close to her heart even as worry coursed through her veins. "But she already told him she didn't want to see him again."

"No worries," Addie said with a dismissive wave. "My mommy says men don't listen very well."

Mickie paused. She'd never heard that before, but it made sense. Aunt Amy had told Uncle Wayne to do lots of things—sometimes in a very loud voice—but he never seemed to do any of them, so maybe Addie was right.

"It has something to do with being a boy," Addie continued. "I don't think their ears work the same as girls."

Mickie thought for a moment. Although Rachel had been looking right at Mr. Rossi when she'd said those horrible words to him Monday morning, he hadn't gotten upset. And today he'd been very nice to both of them.

He acted as if…Mickie's heart picked up speed…as if *he'd never heard Rachel say she didn't want to see him again.*

Mickie trembled with excitement…and relief. There was still hope. Still a chance that she could end up staying in Jackson Hole with Rachel and Mr. Rossi. Still a chance they could be a family.

Rachel pulled into the parking lot of the National Museum of Wildlife Art, wondering if she'd ever really know what made little girls tick. Since Mickie had first come to stay with her, Rachel had tried to interest the ten-year-old in going through the museum without success. Then two minutes ago they were driving down

Highway 89 when the girl practically jumped out of her seat insisting she really, really, really wanted to stop.

"It's a cool place." Rachel stepped from the vehicle. "I think you'll like—"

"C'mon," Mickie called, already halfway up the sidewalk. "Let's get inside."

Although the air held a bite, it wasn't *that* cold. Still Rachel hustled inside. Once she'd paid for their admission, Mickie grabbed her hand and pulled her along. "There's someone, ah, *something* we need to see."

Rachel stopped, now thoroughly confused. "You've never been here. How do you even know what you're looking for?"

Mickie hesitated. "Addie comes here with her mom and dad all the time."

Ah, now it made sense.

"Honey, just because Addie saw something here doesn't mean we'll be able to see it, too. They have what are called 'traveling' exhibits that—"

"If I didn't know better I'd think you two were following me."

Rachel's breath caught in her throat at the familiar baritone. She whirled. "Derek."

She'd expected to see paintings and photographs and bronze sculptures in the beautiful building made of native rock. She hadn't expected to see him. For whatever reason, Mickie didn't seem as surprised.

He rocked back on his heels looking incredibly appealing in his dark pants and a sweater. "What brings you here on a Thursday afternoon?"

After her conversation with her friends, Rachel had considered calling him, but that seemed more of a "I want a relationship with you" than "I want to be friends." She'd hoped they'd run into each other. Now that they had, she wasn't going to blow the opportunity.

"Mickie wanted to see an exhibit that Addie mentioned to her." Rachel smiled warmly. She should tell him she'd changed her mind. This was the opportunity. But the desire coursing through her veins at his nearness was...disturbing. The reaction seemed a little too strong for a *friend*.

Derek shifted his attention to Mickie. "What exhibit did you come to see?"

The girl took a step to the side and pointed in no specific direction. "Just, ah, one back there. I'll look for it while you and Rachel talk."

She slipped past him and didn't stop or turn around even when Rachel called her name.

"Kids." Rachel shook her head and chuckled.

"It's a great museum. I enjoyed going through it." He glanced at his watch.

"Are you leaving?" She did her best to keep the disappointment from her voice.

"I'm skiing Snow King at one-thirty."

"With Travis?"

"Actually a friend is in town for the day and wanted to get together." His voice took on a teasing tone. "I do have more than one friend, you know."

Rachel swallowed past the sudden lump in her throat. "Boyfriend? Or girlfriend?"

"Matt and I played ball together in college."

Although she told herself it didn't matter, her knees went weak with relief.

He stared expectedly as if waiting for her to hit the conversational ball he'd pitched.

Have you missed me? she wanted to ask. *Do you wish we were still friends?* But she told herself not to rush. Ease into those questions. She clasped her hands together. "So, how've you been?"

"Since I saw you at the grocery store?" His blue eyes twinkled. "I've been good. Yourself?"

Missing you. "Just peachy."

Dear God, had she really said *peachy?*

Derek grinned. "Sounds like you've been especially good. Or maybe it's just that I'm hungry."

She met his gaze and familiar electricity engulfed her. Rachel now understood her hesitation, why she hadn't told him she wanted to be friends. It wasn't the friendship she was worried about, it was this physical attraction, this chemistry between them.

He gently touched her hand.

The skin turned hot beneath his fingers.

"Tell Mick goodbye for me?"

"Of course." Rachel couldn't believe he was leaving. She couldn't believe she was letting him go. "I'll see you around."

He winked. "I'm convinced it's inevitable."

And then he was gone.

Rachel found Mickie toward the back of the museum, her head tilted to one side, staring at an oversize portrait of a buffalo.

The child's green eyes lit up when she saw Rachel. But her smile quickly turned to a frown. "Where's Mr. Rossi?"

"He left." Rachel tried not to let her own disappointment show. "He was heading out to Snow King to ski."

"We could go with him." The words tumbled from the child's lip one after the other. "I'm lots better than I used to be and—"

"Honey." Rachel gently placed a hand on the child's shoulder, stilling the stream of words. "He already had plans with someone."

Mickie turned pale. "With a girl?"

"A guy he used to play baseball with," Rachel said, wondering why it mattered to Mickie. "He was running late, but wanted to make sure I told you goodbye."

"Is he coming over later?" she pressed.

I wish.

Rachel shook her head, not trusting her voice.

Mickie glanced at the floor. When she looked up, her lips dropped like a sad little clown. "I don't feel so good. Is it okay if we go home?"

Even though they'd just arrived, Rachel didn't mind leaving. She was feeling kind of sick herself. She'd had her chance to tell Derek she wanted to be his friend, but she'd choked.

Even though he'd appeared confident that their paths would cross again, Rachel wasn't convinced. She had the feeling she'd blown her opportunity. And she'd learned a long time ago that sometimes there are no second chances.

After the conversation with Rachel at the wildlife museum, Derek spent the rest of the day trying to put her out of his head. She'd been a thousand times friendlier than she'd been at the grocery store. In fact, for a second he had the distinct impression she'd changed her mind and now wanted to be friends.

But that was probably wishful thinking.

The pointless speculation didn't end on the slopes. When he got home he kept his phone close to make sure he didn't miss a call or a text from her. She knew how to reach him. While decorating his tree the other night, they'd gotten silly. She'd programmed her number into his phone and he'd put his in hers.

By the time he went to bed he'd *almost* convinced himself that he should make the overture. Thankfully, the next morning he felt stronger. When his resolve to let her set the pace once again began to waver, he made plans to meet Travis at Jackson Hole resort. Yet when he passed the bunny slope, he remembered Mickie's first successful run. And when he and Travis hit the expert slopes, all he could think of was the joy on Rachel's face when they'd skied together.

"Interested?" Travis asked as they walked toward the lodge.

"Yes," Derek said. There was no use lying any longer. He *was* interested in Rachel. Very interested.

"Even if you don't like karaoke, there are lots of pretty women," Travis said. "Not to mention cold beer. And the best pepperoni pizza in Jackson."

Derek cocked his head. "Huh?"

"Willy's Place. Cheap draws. Great pizza. Hot women. You in?"

Derek smiled. Right now he was more interested in hot pizza than hot women. Still, if a little feminine conversation would take his mind off Rachel, he was all for it.

* * *

Rachel glanced at the clock on her living-room wall while Mickie added up how much Rachel owed her for landing on Boardwalk. The little girl was a Monopoly tycoon. She'd put hotels on her many properties and giggled every time Rachel's "iron" landed on one of them. But occasionally she'd turn quiet and a look of sadness would fill her eyes. That was when Rachel knew that Mickie was missing a certain former baseball player.

Rachel massaged her temples.

"You okay?" Mickie reached over and took the play money she was owed from Rachel's dwindling stash.

Rachel forced a smile. "Just a bit of a headache."

Mickie's gaze searched hers. "I miss him, too."

Although Rachel kept the smile on her face, she was sure it looked as frozen as it felt. While talking with Derek at the museum she'd done her best to be open and approachable. But then she'd gotten scared. Scared he'd want more than she could give. Scared friendship wouldn't be enough for her either.

"Why don't you call him?" Mickie suggested.

Rachel moved her fingers from her temples to massage her equally tense neck muscles.

Mickie's gaze narrowed. "You don't look good."

Rachel shrugged.

"Aunt Amy used to get a lot of headaches. Especially when Uncle Wayne was home." Mickie thought for a moment. "She'd lock herself in the bathroom and take a bubble bath. By the time she unlocked the door, Uncle Wayne had left with his friends and her headache had floated away on a bubble. I bet it could help you, too."

"Perhaps later," Rachel said, although a steamy tub

filled with bubbles did sound appealing. "First we need to pick up the game and—"

"No worries. I'll do it," Mickie said, sounding almost eager.

By now the vise around Rachel's head had tightened and her head was pounding. "Sure you don't mind?"

"It'll be fun." Mickie slung an arm around the neck of the bloodhound who had stayed close to her side all night. "Fred will help me."

"Well, I thank you both." Rachel rose to her feet and reached for her phone.

Quick as lightning, the child's hand closed over it. "Why don't you leave it here? That way if anyone calls I can answer it while you're in the bathtub."

Rachel pulled her brows together. "Who'd be calling this late at night?"

"Maybe Mr. Rossi." Mickie scrambled to her feet, her expression anxious.

Rachel sighed. To have the faith of a child… "I'll leave it. But, honey, if he was going to call, he'd have done it by now."

"Maybe he will. Maybe he won't." But the look on Mickie's face said the girl still had hope.

Ignoring the pounding in her head, Rachel pulled the girl into her arms and held her close. "It's no big deal, Mick. You and me, we have fun, just the two of us."

To her surprise, Mickie didn't pull back. Instead, she rested her head against Rachel's chest. "I love you."

The words were so soft Rachel wondered if she'd only imagined them. She tightened her hold on the child. "I love you, too."

Mickie lifted her head, her green eyes large. "Does that mean you're going to keep me?"

Rachel wanted to weep at the bald hope in the child's eyes. She'd already made an appointment to meet with Mickie's social worker after the Christmas holidays to see what adopting Mickie would entail. But for now Rachel wouldn't make promises she wasn't sure she could keep.

"I'd love to keep you. But you deserve a mom *and* a dad."

"But I want *you*."

Rachel's heart rose to her throat. The words she wanted so badly to say, the promise she longed to give, stood poised on the tip of her tongue. But what if the social worker said Rachel couldn't adopt Mickie? No, now was not the time.

"You'll have a family soon," Rachel said instead. "I know you will."

"I will have a family," Mickie said with a determined gleam in her eyes. "And we're going to be so happy. You just wait and see."

Chapter Eleven

Derek leaned back on his bar stool and took a sip of beer. While Travis lived close enough to the downtown bar to walk home, he had to drive. That was why he was still on his first and only round.

Travis had been right about this place. Not only did it have an abundance of Western charm with its mahogany bar, beveled glass mirror and sawdust on the rough wood floor, but also the pizza was great, the beer cold and the women beautiful.

The young doctor appeared to be a regular here. He'd been warmly welcomed not only by Willy— the bartender and proprietor—but also by the entire waitstaff.

Derek cracked open a peanut shell. "I like it here."

"Everyone likes Willy's Place." Travis added a small can of tomato juice to his beer. "Even M.K."

"Speaking of Mary Karen, what's up with the two of

you?" Derek didn't like to pry into another man's business, but there was such heat between them that Derek was surprised they didn't self-combust when they were in the same room.

"We're friends." Travis shrugged, his gaze scanning the crowded bar. "We go way back."

"Did you two ever date?"

Travis shifted on his bar stool to face Derek. "What is this? Twenty questions?"

Ah, he'd hit a nerve. "Just curious."

"We hung out for a while when she was in college," Travis said. "Then she met Mr. Wrong, got married, had the boys. The jerk left her right before Logan was born."

Derek shook his head. No one seeing Mary Karen's ready smile and cheerful nature would guess her life had been anything but perfect.

"She's a pretty woman." Derek took a sip of beer. "Why'd you let her get away?"

"She wanted kids." Travis's eyes took on a faraway look. "I didn't."

"You still feel that way?"

"Don't sound so surprised. Lots of people are perfectly happy without rug rats underfoot." Travis's gaze narrowed. "But not you, eh, Rossi?"

Taking a sip of beer, Derek calmly held Travis's stare.

"In fact, you want 'em with my pretty nurse."

Derek kept the smile on his lips. He even managed a laugh. "Children with Rachel? I barely know her."

"You're hot for her."

"Like you are for Mary Karen," Derek said easily. "That doesn't mean you want kids with her."

Travis chuckled. "You've got that right. I did my time, raising my brothers and sisters. Now I steer clear of any woman with the home-and-family vibe." His gaze shifted. "That's why I like the Norland twins."

The doctor gestured to two leggy blondes stepping off the karaoke stage. "All they're looking for is fun."

The girls, er, women, caught Travis staring and waved. He motioned and they started across the room. With tight-fitting blue jeans and stretchy sweaters that emphasized their considerable assets, the sisters were every red-blooded male's fantasy.

Unlike Rachel's hair, which was the color of honey, the long, straight strands hanging down the twins' backs were silvery platinum. Their eyes were large and a startling violet blue.

The sultry scent of their perfume reached Derek even before the girls shimmied through a group of cowboys to stand so close that their "assets" pressed against his arm.

"Hey, Travis." The blonde gazed at the young doctor through lowered lashes. "We haven't seen you around lately."

"Not enough hours in the day, ladies." Travis flashed a smile and introduced the first blonde as Tiffany, and the other as Kimmie.

"We know Derek." Tiffany exchanged a look with Kimmie and they both giggled. "He's been in all the tabloids."

"If you were my man, I'd never let you go." Kimmie

leaned close and slid a hand up Derek's leg. "And I guarantee you'd never want to let *me* go."

Between Jenna and Heather, his first two fiancées, this had been the kind of woman Derek had sought out: beautiful, sexy and looking for one thing—a good time.

"Any man who'd let you go would have to be a fool, Kimmie." Travis met Derek's gaze, his eyes twinkling with humor. "I don't *think* my friend here is a fool."

Kimmie leaned forward and unexpectedly kissed him on the mouth. Her lips were soft and warm and the kiss was…pleasant. But that was all. Not a single spark.

"Whaddayasay, Mister Baseball Man? Your place?" Her voice was low, sultry and extremely sexy.

Derek knew he only had to smile and Kimmie would be in his bed. Call him a fool, but that was not what he wanted—or rather *who* he wanted.

The "no" had already started to form on his lips when his cell phone buzzed, indicating a new text.

"Excuse me a moment." He pulled the phone from his pocket. "I need to get this."

There was no reason to read the text this second, other than checking it would give him time to figure out a tactful way of turning down Kimmie.

The text was simple and to the point.

I miss u. Call me.

Derek read it three times. Blood coursed through his veins like an awakened river. Although there wasn't a name at the end, he recognized the number, remembered clearly Rachel programming it into his phone.

He stood, gently dislodging Kimmie from his arm. "I have to leave."

Tiffany, who'd just downed her second Jell-O shot in as many minutes, looked up in surprise. "Is someone having a baby?"

Derek stared, confused by the odd response.

Kimmie rolled her eyes but laughed good-naturedly. "You are so drunk."

Then Tiffany began to laugh. Only hers was a loud "look at me" kind of laugh that made most of the men in the room glance her way. "Ohmigosh, I got you mixed up with Travis and his baby business."

"You've had a lot to drink," Kimmie said.

Tiffany slanted a glance at Travis. "You deliver babies. That's what you do. Right?"

"Thanks for remembering," Travis said with a wry smile.

"Are you sure you have to go?" Kimmie's lips formed a perfect pout. "We were just getting acquainted."

"It was nice meeting you both," Derek said, his mind already calculating travel time. Regardless of the route he took, he should be at Rachel's in twenty.

"Everything okay?" Travis asked in a low tone.

"Home and hearth call," Derek said.

Understanding filled Travis's eyes. "Be careful. Don't do anything I wouldn't do."

But the words barely registered. Derek had already started for the door, visions of a warm welcome dancing in his head.

Derek made it to Rachel's townhome in fifteen minutes. He told himself it didn't make sense to be so excited about a simple text. Still, the little he knew about Rachel told him that her reaching out to him was a big deal.

He covered the distance to her front door in several long strides. By the time he reached the stoop, he'd made a decision. He wouldn't mention the text. She said she missed him and he'd come. No need to make a big deal out of it.

Derek straightened his shoulders and lifted a hand. Before he could knock, the door flew open. But instead of Rachel, Mickie greeted him with a warm smile.

"Hey, Mick, it's good to see you."

"Don't worry, I'm going to bed." She motioned him inside. "That way you and Rachel can be alone."

Not quite sure how to respond to that comment, Derek stepped inside. He pulled the door shut behind him, his gaze scanning the living room. Fred sat alone in front of the fire. The bloodhound thumped his tail when Derek's gaze settled on him. "Where's Rachel?"

"She's just getting out of a bubble bath."

Derek's heart sank. When he'd gotten the text, he'd assumed she wanted to see him. But come to think of it, she'd said "Call me," not "I need you now." At the very least he should have called before rushing over.

He reached back for the doorknob. "I'll stop by tomorrow. Or call."

Mickie grabbed his coat sleeve. "Don't even think about leaving."

Derek raised a brow.

She flushed. "It's just that Rachel would be so disappointed if I let you go. She *really* wants to see you. More than anything."

Derek's spirits rose. Perhaps he hadn't misunderstood the tone of the text after all.

"Mickie," Rachel's voice came from down the hall. "Who's there?"

"Mr. Rossi," the little girl yelled. "He missed you as much as you missed him."

A strangled sound came from the hall. Derek grinned.

"I'll be right there," Rachel called out. "Let me just pull on some clothes."

"No need to get dressed on my account," he said.

"She *has* to get dressed, silly goose." Mickie rolled her eyes. "You wouldn't want her to come out here *naked,* would you?"

"Certainly not," Derek said when he realized she expected a response. The trouble was, he'd already begun to envision Rachel greeting him sans clothes. It was a potent image.

"Fred and I are tired. We're going to bed," Mickie said, then paused. "Rachel's not tired at all."

"Good to know." Derek tousled her hair as she walked by. "Sleep well."

The child lifted her eyes to his. "We're happy you came over tonight."

Derek smiled and shrugged off his coat. He'd just picked up the television remote when Rachel appeared in the doorway. The ends of her hair were damp. Her feet were bare. Dressed in a long-sleeved T-shirt and worn blue jeans, she looked simply delectable.

He realized he was staring when her cheeks turned a lovely rose color.

"I didn't mean to make you hurry out of your bath."

A smile teased the corners of her lips. "Are you

kidding? You saved me from turning into a prune. Besides, it's good to see you."

At that moment, Derek realized his analysis of the text had been spot-on. Whatever reservations she'd had about his being her friend had been put to bed.

"Can I get you a glass of wine?" she asked. "Or a cappuccino?"

"Cappuccino?"

She laughed. "I bought a cappuccino maker at a yard sale last summer. I confess I haven't used it much. Actually, I haven't used it at all."

He loved seeing her so lighthearted. "Then we should break it in."

Derek stood back while Rachel dug the machine out from the back of the cupboard. Once it was on the counter, she tossed him the instruction book and asked that he read it to her. When she began tamping the grounds, he murmured words of encouragement and retrieved a carton of milk from the refrigerator.

Placing the carton on the counter, he peered over her shoulder and breathed in the intoxicating scent of her. She smelled like sweet strawberries and rich coffee.

She didn't seem to notice that he wasn't fully focused on the process. Making a simple cup of cappuccino appeared to demand her total concentration.

"I've mastered the machine." She turned, her cheeks flushed with triumph. "A few more minutes and you'll have the best cup of cappuccino ever."

"I don't care about coffee."

He took a step closer and Rachel's breath caught in her throat. Derek stood so near that she could see the tiny flecks of gold in his blue eyes.

"Not coffee…cappuccino," she murmured, her heart picking up speed.

His gaze dropped to her mouth. "Whatever."

Rachel wasn't sure what had made him stop over tonight, but she was suddenly oh so glad he'd come.

"I want to be your friend," she confessed, stumbling over the simple words.

"I know." His hands settled on her hips. "I missed you, too."

Rachel's thoughts swirled. Had she said she missed him? Out loud? The spicy scent of his cologne coupled with his nearness made it difficult to remember. But stepping back didn't cross her mind. Standing in the warm glow of the kitchen with him felt right. She twined her fingers together behind his neck.

A tiny niggle of guilt rose up, but she shoved it aside. Like Lexi had said, lots of men and women were friends. And, according to July, sometimes those friends even… kissed.

The look in Derek's eyes told her that was exactly what he wanted to happen. But he remained still and waited.

He'd made the first move by showing up. The next was up to her. Rachel gathered her courage and covered his mouth with hers. She didn't linger particularly long, but it didn't matter.

Her mouth had barely left his when Derek began scattering kisses across her face and down her neck. She arched her head back giving him full access to the sensitive expanse of her neck and shoulders.

He took full advantage.

"Ah, Derek," she breathed his name.

His lips returned again and again to her mouth. Even though it was below freezing outside, the kitchen air turned steamy.

Rachel opened her mouth to him and he slipped his tongue inside. She was already reeling when his hand slipped under her shirt and closed over her bare breast. She gasped when he flicked his thumbnail over the tip, then pushed aside her shirt and his mouth closed over the rosy tip.

An ache of longing began from her innermost core and quickly spread throughout her body. Dear God, she'd forgotten how good a man's touch felt.

She was praying he wouldn't stop when a loud woof broke through her passionate fog. Rachel jerked from Derek's arms, yanked her shirt down, then listened to the click-clack of toenails on the hardwood.

Derek shoved his hands into his pockets and rocked back on his heels. "Fred?"

Combing a shaky hand through her hair, Rachel nodded, wondering how they could go from passionate to awkward in less than sixty seconds. That had to be one for the record books.

"He sure disappeared quickly this evening," Derek said, apparently deciding to fill the silence.

"He goes to bed early these days," Rachel said. "Mickie wears him out."

The dog now stood at the edge of the kitchen. Was that censure Rachel saw in his big brown eyes? Or amusement?

"Do you think he knows what was going on?" Derek asked in a melodramatic whisper.

The question was so over-the-top that Rachel chuckled

and played along. "Of course. Bloodhounds are smart dogs."

Derek held out his hand, but Fred headed back the way he'd come. "I thought Mickie might make an appearance," he said as the dog turned the corner toward the bedrooms. "But she must still be sleeping."

"Thank goodness." Rachel met his gaze. "Next time we'll have to be more careful."

Next time? Why had she just given him the impression there would be a next time? Rachel opened her mouth to tell him there would be no replay—instant or otherwise—but the words wouldn't come.

After all, what was the harm in a little friendly kissing—a touch now and then—between friends? So they'd rounded second base. That didn't mean she had to head for third. And while Derek may have hit many home runs in his career, that wasn't happening with her.

She had no intention of sliding into home plate with the sexy ballplayer. No intention at all.

Chapter Twelve

Fun of the sexy kind wasn't on Rachel's mind the next day. Christmas shopping was the name of the game. Before Derek had left her house, he'd asked if he could see her again. She'd promptly invited him to go Christmas shopping with her and Mickie.

But a last-minute invitation to go tubing at Snow King with Addie and her family had changed Mickie's plans. So now it was just her and Derek and the Big Box store on Highway 89.

Derek wheeled the Escalade into the drive and slowed to a crawl. Rachel couldn't recall when she'd seen the parking lot so packed.

By the time they found a parking spot and reached the entrance, Rachel was wondering if this had been a mistake. Then she walked through the front door and was mesmerized.

A group of high school students, dressed like

characters from *A Christmas Carol,* were singing songs from the show while parents handed out leaflets advertising the upcoming high school production.

When the students began to sing "A Place Called Home," Christmas spirit—so long absent—found its way into Rachel's heart.

"I wish Mickie were here." She smiled and waved at the young boy dressed as Tiny Tim.

"Don't you think she's too young for a boyfriend?" Derek asked.

"Boyfriend?" Rachel gasped. "I meant she'd enjoy the singing and the costumes."

Before he could respond, a group of teenage boys came charging by them on their way out of the store, laughing and shoving each other. Derek wrapped a protective arm around her shoulder and pulled her close, shielding her body with his.

"Thank you."

He winked. "My pleasure."

A flood of warmth slid through Rachel's veins. How long had it been since she'd had a man to protect her?

Protect her? Rachel laughed out loud. She was a grown woman. Independent. Hoping to adopt a child one day soon.

"Something funny?" Derek asked, accepting a cart from a woman in a blue smock.

Rachel wasn't sure how to answer. Then she decided you could never go wrong with the truth.

"Having you step between me and those boys, it was…nice."

"So what was funny?" The sweetness of his gaze

made her wonder what *had* been so funny. But she'd gone too far to turn back now.

"I found myself thinking how long it had been since I'd had someone to protect me. Then I realized how ridiculous that was." Her words came quicker as the smile slipped from his lips. "This is the twenty-first century, not the nineteenth. I don't need a man to protect me."

He didn't respond immediately and Rachel wasn't sure what else to say. She felt as if she'd just dug a big hole and now stood teetering, ready to fall in.

"At the risk of sounding sexist," he said at last, "I *want* to protect you and keep you safe."

"Even if I'm more than capable of doing that myself?" Her voice came out sharper than she'd intended. But the terror that had gripped her when Tom had died wasn't easily forgotten. He'd been her rock and then suddenly she'd been alone. Until then, she'd never realized how much she'd depended on him. She'd survived, but it hadn't been easy.

His gaze searched her face and a tiny smile returned to his lips. "You're a strong woman, Rachel. I have no doubt you can handle whatever life throws at you."

She felt the tenseness leave her shoulders. He understood.

"Still, I want to protect you."

The unexpected admission was like a splash of cold water. "What?"

He wheeled the cart into an aisle filled with clothes for preteens, then stopped. "While I know that women, that *you*, can manage just fine, I'm a man. That means I protect those I care about. I want to make things easier for you…if you'll let me."

She swallowed past the sudden lump in her throat. "I want to make things easier, better, for you, too."

He reached over and squeezed her arm. "You already do. Just by being here with me."

Not only the words, but also the sincerity, touched her heart. Impulsively she reached over and took his hand.

"Rachel—"

She met his gaze, the heat in his eyes stoking the fire simmering in her belly.

He took a step closer and cupped her face with his hand.

Rachel held her breath.

"Aren't you Derek Rossi?"

Muttering an expletive under his breath, Derek turned, a smile on his face.

A middle-aged woman with tightly permed hair stepped close holding out a ball cap. "My youngest son is a huge fan. Would you mind signing this cap for him?"

Although Rachel knew Derek hadn't welcomed the interruption, she stood back and listened, amazed at his kindness and patience as he chatted with the woman and signed the cap.

"You were so nice to her," Rachel said, after the mother of his "biggest fan" walked off with a big smile on her face.

"Growing up, I approached my share of ballplayers," he said. "I remember how I was treated. Usually good. Occasionally not. I vowed that when I made it to the show I'd always be there for my fans."

Rachel was impressed. Despite the recent bad press, it appeared Derek Rossi was a genuinely nice guy.

Too good, Rachel thought irritably. It would be easy to fall in love with such a man.

By the time they finished buying a cartful of clothes and toys for Mickie, Rachel's fear had turned to terror. She was having way too much fun with this guy.

Of course you are, she told herself. *He's a friend. That's what you do with friends. You have fun.*

Sometimes you kiss. Sometimes you even hop in bed with them.

Try as she might, Rachel couldn't purge the words from her head. But it wasn't the kissing that occupied her thoughts, it was…the other.

The taste of his lips, the feel of his touch, had released a firestorm of desire.

Was Lexi correct? Could you make love with a friend and neither of you walk away hurt? And what about Tom? She could not, would not, betray Tom. But would it be a betrayal if there was no love involved? If it was just sex?

"Earth to Rachel."

She looked up and realized they were at his Escalade.

"Where to from here?" While waiting for her answer, he clicked open the trunk release and loaded the sacks inside. "If you're hungry we could stop somewhere for lunch."

Her gaze searched his face. In less than two weeks he'd be gone…forever. There could be no happily-ever-after with this man. And that was just fine with her.

"Let's go to my place," she said, feeling bold and more than a little reckless. "Mickie won't be home until five."

He shrugged. "Okay."

By his response he obviously hadn't gotten the message. So Rachel waited until he shut the trunk, then she kissed him. Right out in the parking lot for anyone to see.

Surprise lit his eyes, even as a pleased smile lifted his lips. "What was that for?"

"Does there have to be a reason?"

"Absolutely not."

She turned to step into the Escalade when he spun her around and kissed *her*. By the time he let her go, she was out of breath.

"Well," she said. "That was…nice."

He grinned. Seconds later, Rachel found herself humming to the radio as he turned onto the highway.

"With Mickie not home," Derek said, "it'll be a good time to get her gifts wrapped."

"If we have time. We might be too busy."

"What else would we be doing?"

"No child in the house. The two of us alone." She gazed at him through lowered lashes. "You do the math."

Derek carried the packages into Rachel's townhome, his mind racing. Had she really just asked him to have sex with her?

He was almost certain Rachel hadn't been with a man since her husband died. Although she had a lot of friends, he knew she'd been lonely. If he slept with her, would he be taking advantage of that loneliness? Probably.

Derek decided he should drop off the sacks and make an excuse why he couldn't stay. But by the time he'd placed the bags on the dining-room table, Rachel had already removed her coat and pulled down the shades. With a push of a button, a fire glowed in the hearth. When she held out a bottle of wine, he realized Rachel clearly had her plans set for the afternoon.

"Some wine?" The slight tremor in her voice told him she wasn't as confident as she appeared.

"I'd love a glass." He knew it was the correct response when the lines of worry between her brows disappeared.

She sat the bottle down and held out her hand. "First let me take your coat."

He slipped off his jacket and placed it in her hands, his fingers brushing hers.

A bolt of fire shot up his arm. His eyes met hers and the heat in her blue depths told him she'd felt the electricity, too.

"I'll pour," she said. But the bottle remained where she'd placed it.

"Wine isn't really what I want right now."

"Me neither." Rachel took a step forward, the bold look in her eyes reassuring him, telling he'd been right to stay. This wasn't a woman succumbing to loneliness. This was a woman who knew her own mind, a woman seizing the moment, a woman finally willing to let go of the past and take a chance on the present.

Derek was determined to make this experience

wonderful for her. He would give her no reason to look back with regret. "Are you protected?"

Her blank look sent red flags popping up.

"Are you on something?" he clarified. "I don't have any condoms with me and I don't want you, er, us, to have any pregnancy worries."

A tiny smile lifted her lips, though the look in her eyes remained serious. "No worries. I've got that base covered."

"Good." He tugged her toward him, linking his arms lightly around her waist. "Tonight is going to be perfect."

"Perfect?" Rachel chuckled, a low sexy sound from deep in her throat. "You're setting the bar pretty high, mister."

"Because of you." His voice was husky, barely recognizable. "You deserve perfect."

"I don't need perfect," she said, her eyes dark with need. "I need you."

He tilted his head.

"Wait." Color flooded her cheeks in a warm tide. "That didn't come out quite right."

Derek fought to keep a smile from his lips at her distress. "Low standards. High standards. What matters is you want me."

"I *do* want you, Derek." Her hand cupped his face. "But I'm a little…scared. I haven't been with a man since T—"

Derek slanted his mouth across hers, stopping the name from being spoken. He accepted that Tom had been a big part of her life. But Tom didn't belong in this room with them.

This was Derek's time, his and Rachel's. Three was definitely a crowd.

"There's absolutely nothing for you to be concerned about." His hand flattened against her lower back, drawing her up against the length of his body. "You'll set the speed."

Rachel's heart skittered in her chest. She was really going to do this. *They* were going to do this.

He lifted one hand and brushed the hair back from her face with a gentle hand. A look of tenderness filled his eyes. "Remember, we'll take it as fast—or as slow— as you want."

Their eyes met and a smoldering heat flared. She moved her arm so his hand slid down to hers. She gently locked their fingers together.

Should she kiss him? Take off her clothes? Forget this madness?

The testosterone wafting off him in waves made it difficult to think.

"Let's sit for a moment." Rachel pulled him to the sofa, relieved when he dropped down beside her. But once there, the need to say something, to break the tension-fraught silence, pushed at her. A nervous laugh slipped past her lips and she found herself chattering. "This reminds me of when I was in high school and a boy would come to the house. My parents always insisted we sit on the living-room sofa, in plain sight."

"Were they afraid the guy might kiss you? Like this?" Derek's gaze slid from her eyes down to her mouth, and he leaned slowly forward.

Rachel held her breath.

His lips brushed softly over hers, once, twice, with a teasing gentleness that immediately made her want more.

"I think they were more afraid he'd kiss me like this." She pressed her mouth against his, sliding her tongue over his lips.

Derek responded, changing the angle of the kiss, deepening it. The passionate kiss soon had her heart racing. She clung to him with open hunger, her earlier hesitation burned away by the heat building between them. His mouth devoured hers, leaving her trembling with desire when they finally came up for air.

"Wow," he said.

"Double wow."

"I can see now why your parents kept you in sight," Derek teased.

"Kissing wasn't all that worried them." Rachel batted her lashes. She was being shameless, but God help her, she couldn't remember feeling this turned on. "Touching—they absolutely forbade any touching."

"Touching...like this?" Derek placed his hand over the front of her shirt, cupping her breast through the fabric.

His stroking fingers sent shock waves of longing coursing through her body. Rachel swallowed a moan. "I think it was more the skin-to-skin stuff. Stories they'd heard of boys unhooking a girl's bra and—"

"Getting to second base." Before Derek had finished speaking, his hands were under her shirt and the front clasp of her bra hung open. His fingers lifted and supported her yielding flesh as his thumbs brushed across the tight points of her nipples.

Oh, yes. She bit down on her bottom lip to keep from crying out. This was definitely something that would keep a parent with a teenage girl up at night.

"If they were concerned about the touching," Derek said, "I bet they were also worried about this."

He pushed her shirt up, exposing her breasts to the firelight's glow. Desire deepened the blue hue of his eyes. "You are so beautiful."

Just when Rachel thought she was going to have to beg him to touch her, his hands spanned her waist. He ran his palms up along her sides, skimming the curve of her breast. She held her breath. Her nipples stiffened, straining toward the remembered delight of his touch.

He bent his head to take one of her breasts into his mouth. The powerful pull caused every nerve ending to quiver in delight. A desire to give him the pleasure he was giving her rose inside her.

Rachel longed to run her hands over his body and feel the coiled strength of skin and muscle beneath her fingers. She yearned to taste the salty sweetness of his flesh. Most of all, she wanted to feel him inside her. Now.

Once admitted, need became a stark carnal hunger. "Naked," she said.

He lifted her hand to his mouth and pressed a kiss in the palm, letting her feel the soft stroke of his tongue.

"Agreed," he said.

It quickly became a race to see who could get rid of their clothes the fastest. Rachel beat him by several seconds. As a reward, she let her gaze slide over him. Her lips lifted with female appreciation. The lean build, the muscles in his arms and legs sculpted from years of sports, the light dusting of hair on his chest. Her eyes, which seemed to develop a mind of their own, dropped lower.

Rachel swallowed once…and again. Derek was definitely an All-Star.

He cleared his throat.

She jerked her gaze to his face and found him grinning.

"This—" he gestured to their nakedness "—is what parents worry about."

With a thudding heart, Rachel stepped close, placing her hands on his shoulders. She looked into his eyes, her gaze steady. "We're adults. We're alone. And I really, really, *really* want you inside me."

Rachel didn't remember moving, but the next thing she knew, she was in his arms and they were lying on the soft rug before the hearth.

He kissed her lips over and over while one hand cupped her breast and a thumb rubbed across the swollen tips. Fire shot through her, diving down low in her belly. Her heart hammered and her tightly held control unraveled when he substituted his mouth on her breast and moved his hand between her legs.

She caught her breath as he slid two fingers inside. Her muscles tightened around them.

"Oh," she moaned, pressing herself against his hand, wanting more, needing more.

He kissed her again and brought his thumb into play, brushing it lazily back and forth.

Rachel opened her legs wider in an invitation as old as time. "Please, Derek. Please."

She didn't need to ask again. Seconds later, he plunged inside her.

At the first intimate stroke, a shudder raced through her.

He froze. "Did I hurt you?"

"Only in the very best of ways." She looked into his eyes. Her gaze held his. "Don't you dare stop."

He grinned and slowly began to move in and out until the tightness eased and her entire body throbbed with pleasure.

"More," she said in a voice she didn't recognize. "Harder."

He stroked hard and fast and she stretched and undulated in rhythm with him until their bodies were slick with sweat. She loved the way he felt inside her, filling her completely, rubbing her intimately.

The scent of him, the feel of his body was all that mattered. The pressure inside her grew. He must have sensed her mounting need because he pumped harder, faster, until every nerve ending in her body burned like fire.

"I love...the way you make me feel."

Had he spoken? Or had she? Did it matter?

The shuddering began deep inside her midsection and worked its way out. Her thighs trembled, her hands shook. The passion she'd kept buried fireballed. She never felt anything so intense before. A long deep moan vibrated in her throat and she clutched him tighter, wrapping her legs around his hips. She felt Derek's release, heard him cry out her name as he drove deeply inside her one last time.

Still intimately joined, she lay beneath him, wrapped

in his arms while their racing hearts beat as one. Finally she spoke. "I have one question for you."

He lifted a brow.

"Want to do it again?"

He smiled and let his actions be his answer.

Chapter Thirteen

"Not that one." Mickie stood in the doorway to Rachel's bedroom and shook her head. "It makes you look like an old lady."

Rachel gazed into the mirror at the dress she'd pulled on to wear to church. She'd gotten the dark floral print on sale several months ago but hadn't worn it. Because Derek would be escorting them to church, she wanted to look her best.

Old lady.

She stared into the mirror with a critical eye. Perhaps Mickie was right. "Okay, I'll find something else."

"Wear the blue dress. The one made out of that stretchy material," Mickie urged from her position on the bed. "It makes your boobies look big."

"Now why would I care about that?" Rachel asked in surprise.

"Because boys like girls with big boobies," Mickie said. "And you want Mr. Rossi to like you, right?"

"Where did you hear that about boys liking girls with big boob—er, breasts?"

"Aunt Amy used to say that all the time," Mickie said. "She wore those push-up things to make hers look bigger."

Rachel paused. There were so many directions she could take this conversation, but the service started in less than thirty minutes, so she decided to keep it basic. "Honey, what men are really looking for is women who love them for who they are, who will stand beside them in good times and bad. Someone who not only makes their heart beat faster, but who will be their best friend. Understand?"

Mickie appeared to consider the words for several seconds, then shrugged. "You'd better hurry. Mr. Rossi will be waiting for us."

"Give me five minutes." Rachel's fingers flew as she unfastened the floral print, then let it drop to the floor.

"So which dress are you going to wear?" Mickie asked as Rachel opened the closet.

"The one you suggested, of course." Rachel shot Mickie a wink as she pulled the dress from its hanger. "I love the way it makes my eyes look."

Derek cast a sideways glance at Rachel while everyone else was praying. He wondered if she realized how sexy she looked in that blue dress.

It didn't surprise him that his thoughts had turned to sex. Since he'd left her place yesterday, all he'd been able to think about was her, what had happened on that living-room rug…and how he'd almost blown it.

Saying "I love you" would not have been a smart move. She wasn't ready to hear those words from him. And he wasn't sure he was ready to say them.

Letting him get so close had been a huge step for her. Although encouraged, Derek wasn't a fool. The love she felt for her deceased husband hadn't vanished. And she was still wearing Tom's rings. But yesterday it felt as if she'd given him a small slice of herself. It wasn't much, but it was enough to give him hope. Enough to make him believe he had a fighting chance.

From the time he'd picked up his first ball, he'd been a competitor. But this time the prize wasn't a championship or a pennant race—it was her love. Because yesterday he'd realized he didn't just like Rachel, he *loved* her.

That was why losing her wasn't an option.

After church, Rachel and Derek headed straight to The Coffeepot. It seemed odd to walk through the door without Mickie. But the girl had asked if she could ride with Addie and her family to the café. This left Rachel alone with Derek.

"Sometimes I get the feeling that Mickie— No, that's crazy." Rachel chuckled and sat down.

Once she was seated, Derek claimed the chair beside her. "Tell me."

"It's silly."

"Please." He grasped her hand. It was almost as if he'd been looking for an excuse to touch her, which was okay with Rachel. All through church she'd fought to keep her hands off *him*.

"It's like Mickie wanted to give us time alone together," Rachel said when she realized he was waiting for an answer.

Derek brought her fingers to his mouth. "Remind me to thank her."

A shiver of desire traveled up Rachel's spine. The touch brought to mind memories of the pleasure those lips could evoke in other places.

Not that those sensations had ever been far from her mind. In church, his leg pressing against hers had made it difficult for her to concentrate on the sermon. The only words she remembered hearing was that Christmas was about promises fulfilled.

That same pastor had come to visit her after Tom had been killed. He'd promised that God would walk with her through the darkness and pain. He'd assured her that one day she'd be happy again.

Rachel cast a sideways glance at Derek. She was certain Pastor Schmidt hadn't been envisioning her having sex with Derek Rossi when he spoke of happiness. But Derek did make her happy. In bed. And out.

That didn't make her disloyal to Tom. She and Derek were just FWB…friends with benefits. It was as simple as that.

Derek, her FWB, was still holding her hand when the waitress brought their water and coffee. She pulled it from his grasp when her friends—now his friends, too—began trickling in and filling in the seats around the large table. First Lexi and Nick with the girls, then

David and July with baby Adam. Finally Mary Karen and the terrible trio. The waitress had almost made it all the way around the table when Travis strolled in and dropped into the last empty chair.

"You look like hell," David said to his friend.

"We can't say hell," Caleb said.

"We can't say *damn* either," Connor added.

"Unca David is a bad boy," two-year-old Logan said, and the girls giggled.

Mary Karen fixed an admonishing gaze on her brother.

"Sorry," David said, then turned his attention back to Travis. "Let me say it in a different way. You look unwell, friend. Are you feeling ill?"

Laughter rumbled down the table.

Mary Karen lifted a brow.

"Don't you ever get tired of all that partying?"

"Last night was no party." Travis flashed the waitress a smile when she poured him a cup of coffee. "It so happened that three babies decided they wanted to be born within hours of each other and I was on call."

"Were they okay?" Rachel asked, cursing the unexpected shakiness in her voice.

Derek's hand closed over hers.

"Of course." Travis grinned. "Thanks to the superb medical care their mothers received during the delivery."

This time a collective groan rose up.

Nick leaned forward and looked down the table. "Before we order, I have an announcement. I've been given some complimentary passes to *A Christmas Carol* at the high school tonight. If you're interested in going, let me know. I have more than enough tickets for everyone who wants them."

"Derek and I heard some of the actors singing yesterday. They were excellent." Although no one seemed to find anything odd in what she'd said, Rachel paused. *Derek and I.* The words had flowed from her lips so easily that it was scary.

The ease with which Derek had become part of this group was equally frightening. He skied with Travis, and before they'd left church, he'd made plans to meet David, Nick and Travis at Snow King tomorrow afternoon.

It would never have been that way with Tom. Her husband hadn't liked doing things with friends or with other couples. Being with her had been enough. It had been enough for her, too. Until he'd died and she'd discovered how awful it was to be truly alone in the world.

"—I know it's last-minute."

Rachel blinked. She leaned close to Derek, inhaling the intoxicating scent of his cologne. "What did David say?"

"Apparently some Christmas party is off," Derek said in a low tone.

"Why?" she whispered back. She'd been looking forward to David and July's Christmas party for weeks.

Derek shrugged.

Rachel's gaze narrowed as July returned to her seat after a hasty exit to the restroom only moments before.

"Are you feeling okay, July?" Mary Karen asked her sister-in-law.

David and July exchanged a glance. She nodded and he slipped an arm around her shoulders.

"We're pregnant," David said proudly. "Adam will have a brother or sister in late June."

"It was unexpected," July added. "But we're thrilled."

Tears stung the back of Rachel's eyes. Two babies *and* a loving husband. July was indeed blessed.

Derek leaned across the table and shook David's hand. "You're a lucky man."

"Congratulations," Rachel added her well wishes to the others at the table.

"I still don't understand why you're canceling the party," Mary Karen said. "It would be the perfect venue to announce your pregnancy."

"I know, but the fact is I'm not feeling the best," July said, looking slightly green. "The smell of food makes me nauseated, so doing the preparation—or even simply having the smells in the house—would be a real problem."

"Under these circumstances we didn't think it was a good idea to go through with the party," David said firmly. His tone said the discussion was over.

"My house is too small," Mary Karen said. "Or I'd take it over."

"We're in the middle of packing," Lexi said with a rueful smile. "After Christmas we're headed for six months in Dallas."

"Lexi and Nick make their home part of the year in Wyoming and the rest in Texas where Nick's law practice is based," Rachel said, filling Derek in.

"You can use my apartment," Travis said. "But there's not enough room for the kids."

Even though Mickie was at the other end of the table,

Rachel heard her groan. The ten-year-old had been looking forward to the family-friendly party ever since Rachel had told her about it last week.

"We can have it at my place," Derek said. "There's room for everyone who wants to come and, thanks to Rachel and Mickie, it's already decorated for the holidays. All I need is for someone to recommend a good caterer and I'll be set."

"I'll be happy to help," Rachel said. "If you need me, that is."

Derek smiled. "I'll take all the assistance I can get."

"See, honey—" David gave his wife's shoulder a squeeze "—I told you it would be okay."

"Thank you so much." July's gaze shifted from Rachel to Derek. "I hated to back out at the last minute, but—"

"Your health and the health of your baby is the most important thing," Rachel said, fighting off a pang of envy.

"Don't worry about the caterer," Lexi said. "Rachel and I can go shopping for the ingredients tomorrow and between us we'll whip up a feast."

"I'll come over Tuesday and help," Mary Karen said.

"Just don't let her near the food." A lazy grin lifted Travis's lips. "I want to be able to eat it."

Mary Karen stuck her tongue out at him. Her lack of culinary skills were legendary in Jackson Hole.

July brought a finger to her lips, her gaze thoughtful. "You could drop off the children at my house. I could watch them while you're cooking."

"How about we take them skiing with us instead?" Nick said, earning a big smile from Addie. "If it's okay with the other guys."

"Fine with me," David said.

"Don't worry about my boys," Mary Karen said. "Mom is off this week. She can watch them."

"But I want to go skiing with Uncle David and Travis," Connor said.

"Me, too," Caleb called out in such a loud voice that an older couple at a nearby table turned and smiled.

"Me, me, too," Logan added.

A resigned look crossed Travis's face.

"Okay by me," Derek said and Mickie cheered.

"Then it's settled." Lexi smiled at Derek. "Prepare yourself. Tuesday, your house becomes *our* house."

After breakfast everyone scattered. Rachel and Mickie rode home with Derek. With the Escalade's radio tuned to the all-Christmas station, it wasn't long before she, Derek and Mickie began singing a respectable three-part harmony.

Rachel caught Derek's eye during the chorus of one of her favorite Christmas songs and they shared a smile.

He reached over and took her hand. She laced her fingers through his and continued singing about Grandma getting run over by a reindeer.

Rachel heaved a sigh when her town house came into view. She was having so much fun that she hated to see the drive end.

They'd barely pulled to a stop in the driveway when Mickie took Rachel's key and hopped out. She hurried to the front door, eager to see Fred.

Rachel remained in the SUV with Derek. "I need to speak with you about something."

"Will 'I couldn't help myself' work as an excuse?" A smile teased the corners of his lips. "Somehow it seemed wrong not to sing to 'Frosty the Snowman' and 'Rudolph the Red-Nosed Reindeer.'"

"Yes. No. I mean, the singing was great."

Really, was there anything the man didn't do well?

"The hand-holding," he said. "I admit I forgot for a second about Mickie being in the backseat."

"That was no biggie."

His gaze grew puzzled. "Then what?"

"Your offer to host the party."

The joy that had been in his eyes disappeared.

Darn. Darn. Darn.

"This party won't just be a small intimate group of friends," she warned. "David and Mary Karen's parents were planning to come as well as Granny Fern. John and Kayla will still be out of town, but Ron is coming as well as Coraline, Lexi's old boss. People from the hospital have RSVP'ed. The guest list is quite extensive."

Derek leaned back in his seat, seemingly unconcerned. If anything his smile had widened. "The more you talk, the more I realize what a blast this is going to be."

"Didn't you hear what I said? Think of all the people that will be in your house." Tom refused to host a small dinner party. He'd never have gone for a full-fledged Christmas party.

"The More the Merrier is my motto." Derek shot her a wink. "Besides, Christmas parties mean mistletoe."

And for a handsome unattached man like Derek, that

usually meant kissing lots of pretty women. Rachel's heart clenched at the thought. But she told herself who he kissed was not her concern. Derek was a free agent. One night in her bed—or rather on her floor—didn't make him hers, which was why feeling the pinch of the green-eyed monster made no sense.

"Just so you know there won't be many single women at the party." She tried to keep the relief from her voice.

He trailed one finger slowly down her cheek. "Don't you know by now that there's only one woman I want with me under the mistletoe?"

Rachel's lips began to tingle. She moistened them with her tongue and gazed at him through lowered lashes. "I say…who needs mistletoe?"

Mickie let out a war whoop and dropped the front window shade back into place.

She'd noticed the way Derek had smiled at Rachel during breakfast. Then, on the way home, he'd held her hand. It wasn't much, but Mickie had taken those as *very* encouraging signs.

Now they were kissing. And not just the peck-on-the-cheek type of kiss Rachel gave her every night before bed. From what Mickie had been able to see, this was one of those kisses that you saw in the movies. The kind that made you wonder if they were ever going to take a breath. A Barbie-loves-Ken type of kiss.

If Fred wasn't so big she'd pick him up and dance around the room. Instead, Mickie settled for giving him an enthusiastic hug. Then with a glad cry, she began to twirl.

Chapter Fourteen

Derek hopped out of the shower and dived for the phone. He should already be on his way to pick up Rachel and Mickie for this evening's performance at the high school. But he'd decided to work out first. And then he'd had to clean up. Although the show didn't start for over an hour, because there was no assigned seating, Rachel had told him they should try to get there early.

"I'll be there in fifteen minutes."

"I hardly think so—" his mother chuckled "—considering I'm still in Florida."

"Mom." He swiped a towel from the counter and wrapped it around him. "I thought you were someone else."

"Obviously," she said with a little laugh. "Who is she?"

Derek sat on the edge of the bed. "What makes you think it's a she I'm meeting?"

"If it were a man, you wouldn't be concerned about being late."

"Actually I'm going out with a whole group of friends," Derek said, then wondered why he'd felt the need to keep the truth from his mother. "The local high school is performing *A Christmas Carol* and one of the guys got some free tickets."

"That sounds fun." His mother paused. "Is the young lady who didn't want to see you anymore going to be there?"

"Her name is Rachel," Derek said. "And yes, she's part of this group."

"Derek." Somehow his mom managed to infuse a world of disappointment into his name.

"Trust me, Mom, you'll love her," Derek said. "She's incredibly smart and fun and a genuinely nice person. Did I tell you that she's a nurse? And that she takes in foster kids?"

"Honey—"

"Wait." Derek knew what was coming, but he also knew it didn't apply to his feelings for Rachel. "I know you're thinking this is a huge mistake, but the fact is, I love *her*. More than I ever thought possible."

There, he'd said it. Spoke from the heart. Laid it on the table.

"Well, then, honey, I'm happy for you," she said finally.

Derek could tell by her tone that she was still skeptical, but was keeping an open mind.

"I want you to meet her," Derek said. "You have so much in common. Remember how you wore your wedding rings after Dad died? She did the same thing after her husband died. She—"

"Is she wearing the rings now?"

"Yes, but—"

"She's not over him."

The words were a knife to his heart. When they were out, he barely noticed the diamond on her finger. *Probably because she usually wore gloves.* But when they'd made love, he *had* noticed.

That meant nothing, he told himself. He had certifiable proof Rachel was over Tom. She'd waited all this time, saved herself even, for just the right man. And that man was him.

"She was married for four or five years." Derek kept his tone even. "He was murdered. Does anyone ever get over a loss like that?"

"You say you love her," his mother said, not answering the question. "I'd like to know if she loves you."

Although Rachel hadn't said the words, he sensed she did. "Yes. Yes, she does."

Across two thousand miles he heard his mother expel the breath she must have been holding. "Then I'm happy for you. Though I'm not going to pretend that her still wearing those rings doesn't bother me."

"Isn't that hypocritical?" Derek asked. "Because you did the same thing?"

"I took mine off when I was ready to move on."

"Maybe Rachel doesn't want to forget Tom." God, he hated even saying the name.

"I haven't forgotten your father, Derek. I never will. He has a permanent place in my heart. Taking off the rings was my way of saying to myself and to the world that I was open to loving again." She paused.

Even though she couldn't see him, Derek nodded.

"You won't be happy being second in any woman's life," his mother continued. "You experienced that with Heather. I hope that this isn't the same—"

"Mother, stop." Derek jerked to his feet and stalked across the room to the window, his emotions in a tailspin. "I'm fully capable of handling my own love life."

His tone was sharper than he'd intended, but damn it, she didn't know Rachel. She hadn't seen the way Rachel's eyes lit up when he walked into a room. And Rachel had been the one who'd kissed him, who'd emailed him, who'd asked *him* to be a part of *her* life with that simple text.

She'd even been the one to suggest they have sex. He grinned. Of course he hadn't been that hard to convince.

Still, he hadn't pursued her, she'd pursued *him*. As far as he was concerned, that said Rachel was ready to move on. Ring or no ring.

"I'm sorry, honey." His mother's tone turned conciliatory. "You're a smart man. You don't need me second guessing your decisions. I'm excited to meet your Rachel. I assume I'll get that chance at the awards ceremony next month?"

Derek had forgotten all about the program the second week in January. His award for broadcast excellence had thrilled the network execs. Now that he thought about it, this would be the perfect opportunity for Rachel—and Mickie—to meet his family.

"We haven't nailed that down yet," he said, realizing

suddenly that the month was almost over and there wasn't much time left. Not much time at all.

Rachel glanced at the clock on her mantel. "If Mr. Rossi doesn't get here soon, we're going to be late for the performance."

"He'll be here," Mickie said.

Rachel smiled at the confidence in the girl's tone. Derek need look no further than Mickie to find his number-one fan. And tonight, dressed in a plaid skirt and tights topped with a kelly-green sweater, Mickie looked more like a young lady than a child.

Despite knowing the performance was at a high school auditorium, Rachel had dressed up. The cherry-red cashmere wrap dress was a new purchase. Soft against her skin, the garment made her feel festive yet sexy.

When she'd put it on, Rachel couldn't help thinking how easy it would be for Derek to take it off…

Of course he wouldn't be taking anything off tonight. There would be no making love. Not with Mickie in the house.

Making love.

They hadn't made love. She and Tom had made love. Many, many, many times. Because they were in love. While Tom might not have been the most adventurous lover, she'd always been satisfied. More than satisfied.

Rachel slanted a glance to the side table where her wedding picture sat, suddenly needing to see his face.

Her breath caught. "Where is it?"

Mickie looked up from the sofa where she'd been working with Fred on his tricks. "Where's what?"

"My wedding picture." Her frantic gaze slid to the mantel. Her heart rose to her throat. "The one taken on our honeymoon is missing, too."

"They're not missing," Mickie said in a matter-of-fact tone, lifting Fred's paw and shaking it. "I put them away."

"You *what?*" Rachel's voice rose despite her best efforts to control it. "Why would you do something like that?"

Mickie patted the bloodhound on the head, stood and smoothed her skirt. "Because if I were Mr. Rossi, seeing all those pictures of another man would make me uncomfortable."

Rachel took a deep breath and let it out slowly, keeping a tight grip on her anger. "This is my house, Mickie. I can have pictures of my husband in every room if I want."

"He's not your husband." Mickie met her gaze with a belligerence that set Rachel's teeth on edge. "He was your husband. But he's not now. He's dead."

"Put them back," Rachel ground out the order between clenched teeth, her entire body trembling with emotion. "Put them back *now.*"

When Mickie's chin lifted in a stubborn tilt, words—harsh and angry—pushed at Rachel's lips, but she clamped her mouth shut. She took a deep breath and counted to ten. Then she began to count again. She'd made it to seven when her phone rang. She pulled it from her purse, glancing at the readout. "Derek. Hello."

"You sound funny. Everything okay?"

Out of the corner of her eyes she saw Mickie jerk open a rarely used kitchen drawer and pull out two frames. "Fine." Her voice sounded tight even to her own ears. "Where are you?"

"Five minutes away," he said. "I'm looking forward to tonight. It should be great."

Mickie muttered as she slammed the photos back in place.

"Shrine" was all Rachel heard.

"Rachel? Are you there?"

"I'm here," she said. "You're right. We're going to have so much fun."

She hoped that saying it aloud would make it true. Unfortunately the sullen look on Mickie's face told her the odds weren't good.

Once Derek arrived at Rachel's home, it didn't take long to conclude that something was definitely wrong. Although both Rachel and Mickie put up a polite front, the tension between the two continued on the ride to the high school. Oh, they both talked. To him. Not to each other.

Once they reached the auditorium, Mickie attached herself to Addie like a drowning sailor to a life raft.

Rachel's mood seemed to improve during the performance. Although he laid his arm across the back of her seat, he didn't take her hand. The rigid set of her shoulders said she wouldn't welcome the touch.

"Like it?" he whispered when Scrooge had his epiphany.

"I love it." Her eyes shone in the dim light and Derek's spirits lifted.

Yet after the performance, when Mary Karen invited everyone over to her house for hot chocolate, Rachel declined. Mickie cast a resentful look in the direction of her foster mom, but Rachel appeared not to notice.

By the time Derek pulled into Rachel's driveway, he'd had enough. Enough of the tension. Enough of the phony politeness. Enough of feeling caught in the middle. And he knew if the two of them didn't settle this—and settle it fast—Christmas would be ruined.

And Mickie needed to experience a merry Christmas.

So did Rachel.

Derek shut off the engine and turned in his seat. "Who's gonna tell me what's going on?"

"Nothing is going on." The glare Mickie shot Rachel was at odds with her cheery tone. "Everything is fine."

"Mickie and I had a disagreement right before you came over," Rachel said. "But we're over it. Right, Mick?"

"Yeah," Mickie grumbled. "Whatever."

Derek had been a team captain many times during his high school and college days. Even during his pro career, he'd often been pulled into a leadership role. He'd lost track of the number of times he'd helped players settle their differences for the sake of team harmony. "Have you considered talking about it, airing your feelings?"

"She ordered me around like I was some slave." Mickie's eyes flashed green fire. "Didn't really listen to what I had to say. Didn't care about my opinion."

"And *you* didn't care about *my* feelings," Rachel shot back before clamping her mouth shut.

"You two need to talk this out in a calm, rational manner." Derek shifted his gaze from Rachel to Mickie.

"I tried to explain," Mickie said. "She interrupted me. She didn't even try to listen—"

Derek held up a hand stilling the girl's diatribe. "Ground rules. First, you must be completely honest about your feelings. Second, you let the other one talk without interrupting. Third, and most importantly, before you start the discussion you have to hug."

The last rule was a technique his mother had employed during his sister's tumultuous teenage years. It must have worked because his mom and Sarah were very close now.

Rachel reached for the handle but didn't pull the door open. "I'm willing to give it a try."

"Me, too," Mickie said, though her chin was still lifted. She turned to Derek. "Are you coming in?"

"Not tonight," he said. The child looked so distressed that he gave her a reassuring smile. "Tomorrow. Or Tuesday for sure when we go skiing."

"Promise?"

He lifted his hand and tossed up fingers in a long-forgotten salute. "Scout's honor."

Seemingly appeased, the child turned to Rachel. The smile on her lips didn't reach her eyes. "May I have the keys, please, so I can let Fred out?"

"Thank you. I'd appreciate that." Rachel dug in her purse for a second, pulled out the keys, then dropped them onto Mickie's outstretched palm.

Mickie didn't meet Rachel's gaze and couldn't seem to get out of the vehicle fast enough.

Rachel waited until she was out of earshot to speak. "I want you to know that I am capable of dealing with Mickie on my own."

"I realize that." He tugged her to him and wrapped his arms around her, holding her loosely. "I didn't mean to overstep—"

"You didn't. I should never have gotten so angry with her." She rested her forehead against his coat and he planted a kiss on the top of her head. "I'm just sorry we didn't have time to get these issues resolved before you arrived. You didn't deserve to suffer our drama."

"Never mind that. I had a great time." He brushed a strand of hair back from her face. "I always do when I'm with you."

She lifted her head. "Me, too."

Was that a sigh he heard?

"Call me later," he urged. "Let me know how things go with Mickie."

"I will." Rachel reached for her door handle, but before she pushed it open, she turned back. "You know, it's kind of nice."

"What is?"

"Having a man around."

"How did it go?" Derek relaxed his back against the pillow. Instead of sticking his phone on the charger, he'd brought it to bed with him, determined not to miss Rachel's call. He'd been ready to turn out the lights when it rang.

"Good." Her tone had a lilt to it. The strain that had been in her voice earlier had vanished. "By the way, doing the hug was a very good idea."

"Were you able to see her side?"

"Yes," Rachel said. "And I think she understands my feelings better, too."

Derek was curious about the issue that had polarized them, but she didn't volunteer the information and he didn't ask. "Glad to hear it."

"It may sound crazy, but this experience made me realize just how much I want to be a mom."

"It's not crazy at all." Derek smiled into the phone. "I can easily see you with a half-dozen kids playing at your feet."

"Yeah, well, that's not going to happen."

There was an odd catch in her voice. Surely she didn't think she was too old to start a family...

"I'm older than you and I still plan on having a houseful of kids," he said. "It's not too late for either of us."

"You'll be a good dad," Rachel said.

There was sadness in her voice he didn't understand. He found himself wishing she was in bed with him now so he could comfort her. He'd discover what was troubling her and make it better.

Because that was what a man did for a woman he loved.

Chapter Fifteen

Rachel had been grocery shopping with Lexi for almost an hour and it seemed as if every aisle of the large store had at least one seasonal display. Rachel slowed her steps, then stopped when Lexi paused the cart in front of a display of chocolate-covered marshmallow snowmen. Her friend picked up a handful of the brightly wrapped treats and tossed them into the cart.

Rachel smiled. "Don't tell me we're having those for dessert at the party instead of your famous gingerbread with spiced crème anglaise?"

A sheepish look crossed Lexi's face. "These little guys are for me. They're one of my secret passions. Give me Cadbury eggs at Easter and chocolate marshmallow snowmen at Christmas, and I'm happy."

"No faves at July Fourth? Or Thanksgiving?"

Lexi shrugged, a smile teasing the corners of her lips.

"Laugh all you want. I'm sure you have your passions, too."

"Not unless you count Derek Rossi."

"Are you saying… Oh. My. God." Lexi's gaze searched hers. "You slept with him."

"Lex," Rachel hissed. "Keep it down."

"It's just that I'm so jazzed." Even though her eyes still snapped with excitement, Lexi's voice dropped to a conversational level. "When did this…event occur?"

Rachel sighed, knowing Lexi would hound her until she got some details. "Saturday night."

"How was he?" Lexi pressed. "I mean, how was it?"

Rachel thought back to all the times she and Tom had made love. Predictable. Pleasurable. But those words didn't come close to describing Saturday night in front of the fire. "It was…mind-blowing."

"Oh, Rach, I'm so happy for you." Were those tears in Lexi's eyes? "We all love Derek. And you make such a great couple."

It took a second for the words to fully register.

"Couple?" Rachel's heart fluttered like a trapped butterfly in her throat. "Derek and I, we're not a couple. We're simply FWBs. Friends with benefits."

By the look on her face, Lexi obviously wasn't convinced.

"You're the one who said friends can sleep together," Rachel reminded her.

"They can." Lexi's eyes softened. "But we both know that's not what's going on here."

A shiver of unease traveled up Rachel's spine. "I don't know any such thing."

"This is me. The woman who fell in love with a man who didn't even know his own name." Lexi pushed the cart off the main aisle and parked it by a display of holiday cards. "When I realized I was falling in love with Nick, it was scary. But I took a chance and I'm so glad I did."

"I'm happy it worked for you," Rachel said. "But Derek is my friend. That's all."

Lexi heaved a disappointed sigh. "I really thought it was *L-O-V-E* between the two of you."

"Nope. Just *H-O-T S-E-X*."

Lexi laughed and they proceeded to the checkout lane. Once there, Rachel busied herself unloading the cart.

"You sly dog." Lexi chuckled. "When were you going to tell me about the wedding? Were you keeping it a secret until the party?"

Rachel whirled, a carton of whipping cream in hand. "What wedding?"

"Yours." With a Cheshire-cat smile, Lexi gestured to the rack of tabloids.

Rachel gasped. A picture of her and Derek adorned the front cover of one of the papers. A red arrow pointed to her ring finger. She read the headline:

Did Sexiest Player FINALLY Make It to the Altar?

Rachel opened her mouth, but no words came out.

Lexi snatched the paper from the rack and tossed it on the belt. "If you won't give me the scoop, I guess I'll have to get my information elsewhere."

Her friend's voice bubbled with laughter, but Rachel wasn't amused.

The tattooed cashier picked up the paper. After

scanning it, she glanced at Rachel, then back at the paper. "Your new hubby's a hunk. Congrats."

Rachel blinked.

"Just smile," Lexi whispered in her ear. "And tell her we'll drive up for the groceries."

Derek would never have believed skiing with a bunch of children could be so much fun. Even Travis seemed to be having a good time.

When David offered to watch his nephews so Travis could do his own thing, they all expected the sandy-haired bachelor to jump at the chance. Instead, he stuck around and spent the afternoon on the beginner slope helping the twins.

And when the kids begged them to stop at the lodge for hot chocolate with candy canes, Travis surprised them by coming along.

The pleasant afternoon started to unravel when Connor and Caleb grew bored, grabbed their peppermint sticks and began a sword fight. It completely fell apart when, in trying to stop them, Travis's cup of cocoa ended up in his lap.

That was when they all decided to call it a day. But Derek still had to take Mickie to Christmas Eve program practice at church. He couldn't believe she'd turned down Nick's offer to ride with him and Addie.

After buckling her seat belt, Mickie crossed one leg over the other and swung the top leg back and forth. "Thank you for today, Mr. Rossi. It was a blast."

Derek put the truck in gear and smiled. It had been heartwarming to see Mickie laughing and playing in the snow. "You're welcome."

Mickie stared out the window at a passing minivan filled with parents and children.

"It's so not fair," she said with sudden vehemence.

Confused, Derek cast a sideways glance. Were those tears in her eyes?

"I want to stay here. I want to live with you and Rachel. It's all I want. It's all I'll ever want."

Derek's heart gave a lurch. He understood. He didn't want to be without her or Rachel either.

"You understand...there is no Rachel and me." Yet.

"There could be." Mickie stopped swinging her leg and turned in her seat, the tears gone. "You love her, don't you?"

Derek hesitated. "I do. But I'm not sure how she feels."

"I know the problem." Mickie heaved a heavy sigh. *"Tom."*

"She still wears his rings." The words were out of Derek's mouth before he could stop them. Obviously his conversation with his mother had impacted him far more than he realized.

"She still has his pictures all over the house," Mickie added.

"He was her husband," Derek pointed out.

"Was," Mickie emphasized. "She needs to forget him. *You* need to make her forget him."

"The decision to move on is hers alone," Derek said. "I thought her text meant she was ready. I'm not so sure now."

Mickie stared at the floorboard. "So it's hopeless. I go to a group home. You go back to L.A."

"Not so fast." Derek wanted to be with Rachel, but

even if that didn't happen, he still wanted Mickie to be his daughter. Yet he didn't want to give her false hope. "In the past, when I thought about taking in a foster child, I thought I'd have to be married to make it work. And in my mind, the child was always a boy."

"Yeah." Mickie slumped back down in her seat. "Everyone wants a boy."

Derek's gaze settled on this funny, smart, amazing girl.

"Then I met you," he said. "And I wondered how I could have been so foolish."

"Really?"

Derek nodded. "I also met some amazing people who made me realize that life doesn't have to fit into some nice, neat slot."

Mickie's gaze grew puzzled. "I don't understand."

"Mary Karen is raising three small boys on her own. Lexi raised Addie by herself until last year when she met Nick." Derek's resolve to make this situation work strengthened with each word. "If they can do it, I can, too."

Hope lit the child's eyes. "Are you saying…?"

"I want you to be my daughter," Derek said. "Assuming I can get your caseworker's approval, when I return home to L.A., I'd like you to come with me."

The choral director turned his attention to the preschoolers for a second and Mickie scooted over to where Addie stood so she could finish the story she'd started earlier.

"Then he told me he wants me to live in California with him," Mickie said.

"Yippee."

When the choral director shot her a warning glance, Addie smiled sweetly. "I mean, praise the Lord."

"Let's go over here." Mickie took Addie's hand and pulled her across the shiny linoleum of the church basement until they stood behind a large green plant. "I don't know what to do."

"Duh, you go with him. This is what you wanted, remember?"

"I want Rachel, too," Mickie reminded her friend. "And so does Mr. Rossi."

"Hmm." Addie brought a finger to her lips and a thoughtful look crossed her face. "You're right. Who wants half a sundae when you can have the whole thing?"

"Huh?"

Addie leaned close. "You have to figure out how to get the whole sundae."

Mickie paused. Was this a riddle?

"You have to make Rachel see that she loves Mr. Rossi and has to forget all about her husband," Addie said impatiently.

Mickie thought how Rachel had reacted to her putting the pictures of Tom in the drawer. "That's not going to be easy."

"Maybe," Addie said, beginning to twirl. "But just think how great it'll be when you have both a dad *and* a mom."

Chapter Sixteen

The garage door rumbled open and Rachel's heart skipped a beat. Derek had given her the pass code for the gate as well as a house key so she could drop off the groceries for tomorrow night's party. He shouldn't be surprised to see her.

Still, by the time he walked into the kitchen, her heart was thumping like a schoolgirl's. She fumbled with some condiments on the counter, but relaxed a little when his lips widened into a smile.

"I just dropped off Mickie at the church," he said. "I thought you'd already be here and gone. This is a nice surprise."

Even though she'd like to believe otherwise, Rachel knew the warmth rushing through her had nothing to do with the furnace kicking on. "How'd the skiing go?"

"Couldn't have been better. Mickie did fabulous."

"Good to hear." Dear God, could she sound any more tongue-tied and gauche?

His brows pulled together. "Is something wrong?"

"Do you read the tabloids?" Rachel nearly groaned aloud. She'd planned to be casual and offhand about the whole matter, not blurt it out.

"Not usually," he said. "Do you?"

"Only when my picture is on the front page." She gestured to the paper she'd left on the table. "See for yourself."

His frown deepened and he dropped down into a chair.

She stood behind him and peered over his shoulder. "The picture was taken the night we ate at Perfect Pizza."

In the photo she was smiling across the table at him and he was staring into her eyes with that sexy intensity that made her squirm even now.

Derek barely glanced at the photo.

"The interest in me had died down," he murmured to himself as he flipped open the paper and paged until he got to the article. "What could have gotten it stirred up again?"

Assuming the question was rhetorical, Rachel remained silent while he read.

"It's Niki." He shoved the paper aside in disgust. "The article mentions she's up for a role in a movie that's being cast next month. Obviously this is her way of keeping her name out there."

While it appeared to make perfect sense to him, for Rachel the puzzle pieces didn't fit. "She gets free press by making it look like you got married?"

"The fact that I finally married is the article's hook, which is only interesting if you bring up my past," he said in a matter-of-fact tone.

"That's why they included all that information about your former fiancées." Rachel had read the article several times—okay, close to ten. It had been impossible to find a trace of the man she'd come to know over the past few weeks in the slanted piece. Still, there was no denying the fact that Derek had walked away from three women he supposedly loved enough to propose marriage.

"Let me tell you what they got right," he said, his eyes serious and very blue. "And what they got wrong."

"Like I said when we first met, you don't owe me an explanation."

"Yes, I do." His gaze met hers and the depth of emotion reflecting back at her made her heart pound even harder. "Things are different now."

It was true. Three weeks ago they'd barely known each other. Now they were…more.

"According to the article, you're my wife," he said, flashing a grin. "That means you should know the truth."

Without waiting for a response, he stood, took her hand and pulled her to her feet. "First, let's find some place more comfortable to talk."

They'd barely gotten settled on the sofa in front of the fire when he began his story.

"Jenna, my first fiancée, was my college girlfriend. When I got drafted, we discovered that we'd had a miscommunication of sorts. I thought we'd get married and she'd move with me. Came to find out she thought I wouldn't get drafted. She had no intention of leaving Minnesota. It became a stalemate with neither of us willing to give."

"I came to Wyoming with Tom," Rachel said. "Even though I really didn't want to move so far from where I'd grown up."

"That's the difference." A muscle jumped in Derek's jaw. "You loved him. Neither Jenna nor I loved each other enough to make the sacrifice."

The situation seemed more sad than anything else.

"What about fiancée number two?" Rachel asked, when he sat silently staring into the fire. "They say you got cold feet and dumped her at the last minute, leaving her with thousands of dollars of wedding expenses."

Derek pulled his gaze back to her.

"I met Heather when she was on the rebound. I'd have moved anywhere, done anything for her." The flash of pain in his eyes told her more than any words that he'd loved Heather deeply. A stab of jealously lanced Rachel's heart. "But shortly before we were to be married, she came to me in tears and confessed she was still in love with her old boyfriend. She'd made a mistake by agreeing to marry me."

"But all the news reports at the time said *you* broke up with her."

"That was the official story." Derek raked a hand through his hair. His lips twisted in a semblance of a smile. "Her dad was a huge baseball fan. Heather used to tease that he loved me more than he did her. We both knew he'd never forgive her for dumping me. So I took the heat."

Rage at Heather for leading Derek on and then

breaking his heart rose up and spewed out. "What kind of woman—"

"Heather did a brave thing in being honest with me," Derek said simply. "Now Niki on the other hand..."

"Fiancée number three."

He shook his head. "That whole relationship was a big mistake."

Rachel listened attentively while Derek explained. Her outrage grew with each detail. "I can't believe she tried to trap you with a pregnancy."

"She knew how much I wanted children," he said. "It was a brilliant plan."

Derek loved children. Wanted lots of children.

A cold chill washed over Rachel. She shook it off. He hadn't said anything she hadn't already known.

"Let me see if I've got this straight." Rachel paused for a second. "You found out she was a big fat liar and called it off. Now the woman is out to get you."

"Not out to get me. Out to get publicity."

"Same thing." Rachel waved a dismissive hand. "You should tell your story. Expose her for the fraud she is."

"It'd be nice if the world worked that way, but it doesn't." Derek shook his head. "Tabloid journalism isn't interested in truth. They're interested in selling papers. I'm just sorry you got caught up in it. You don't deserve this."

The warmth in his voice, the concern in his eyes said how much he cared.

In that moment Rachel realized she was no better than Heather. Like his second fiancée, she'd led him on. She'd made him believe her heart was free, made him believe they could have a future together.

Derek wasn't a player. He was the marrying kind. That was why she had to end this relationship before it went any further. *Now.* She had to do it now.

But before she could say a word, he took her hands in his.

"Being with you these past couple weeks has meant the world to me." His gaze never wavered from her face. "You're going to be a hard woman to forget."

Relief mixed with disappointment washed over her. The words Rachel had been about to speak died on her lips. *Hard woman to forget?* Although he obviously cared, he wasn't thinking long-term.

Then why tell him goodbye now? In a little more than a week, he'd be gone anyway and her life would then return to the way it had been before. It was a depressing, er, reassuring, thought.

His gaze slid to the vee of her sweater. "What time do you need to pick up Mickie?"

The spicy scent of his cologne teased her nostrils and tiny sparks of electricity filled the air.

Her heart stuttered at the heat in his gaze. "Ah, not until five."

"Well, because our fictitious union has been blessed by the tabloids…" He brought her hand to his lips and kissed each of her fingers. "I was thinking we should do what newly married people do and—"

"Make love." She'd planned to say "have sex," truly she had, but somehow between her brain and her mouth, the message must have gotten scrambled.

"See, we're even thinking alike." He pulled her to her feet and she laughed. "Want to try a bed this time?"

The fire warmed the air and the light from a Tiffany

lamp lent a golden glow to the room. Outside, large flakes continued to fall, adding more fluffy softness to the already-thick blanket of white.

His eyes met hers and Rachel found herself drowning in the liquid blue depths. The world beyond this room ceased to exist. Nothing mattered. Except her. And him. And right now.

Rachel's fingers moved to the front of her shirt. With her gaze firmly fixed on his face, she began unfastening the buttons one by one. "The sofa works for me."

"Sofa sex." Derek's eyes shone with a wicked gleam. "You, my dear, are a woman after my own heart. I love… it."

Her fingers stumbled on the buttons, rattled by hearing *heart* and *love* in the same sentence. But then his mouth was on hers and her fingers were unbuckling his belt. And thinking became impossible.

As she sank to the sofa cradled in his strong arms, Rachel realized it wasn't his heart that would be broken when he left…but hers.

By the night of the Christmas party, Rachel had begun to wonder if she was obsessed. Whenever she was around Derek, all she wanted to do was get naked.

But tonight wasn't about sex, it was about friends and family and celebrating. When Derek asked her to stand with him at the front door to greet the guests, she'd almost said no, worried they'd look too much like a couple. Then she realized she was being ridiculous. Most of the people coming to the party were strangers to Derek. It only made sense that there was a familiar face at the door to buffer the initial awkwardness.

Only after the guests had begun arriving did Rachel realize Derek would have done fine on his own. Like now, he stood conversing with David and Mary Karen's parents as if he'd known them his whole life.

"Thanks for being here with me," Derek said to her after the couple walked off in search of a glass of wine.

"I'm not doing anything special except stand here," Rachel demurred.

"I strongly dis—" His words were cut off when Ron appeared at the door.

One of the staff Derek had hired for the evening whisked away Ron's coat, but the older man kept a firm hold on his bottle of champagne. He greeted Rachel with a hug, then pumped Derek's hand in an enthusiastic shake before handing him the bottle.

"Congratulations," Ron said. "The wife and I were having breakfast at The Coffeepot yesterday when we heard the news."

Rachel exchanged a glance with Derek. He shrugged and she refocused on Ron. "What news?"

Ron grinned. "Heard you two got hitched."

Derek groaned. "The tabloid article."

Rachel placed a hand on Ron's sleeve and, with a bit of dramatic license, paraphrased Mark Twain. "I regret to inform you that the reports of my marriage are greatly exaggerated."

The older man cocked his head. "Huh?"

"We're not married," Derek said. "There was an article in a supermarket tabloid that suggested that, but it isn't true. Though I admit it did fool a lot of people. In fact my mother and sister saw the article and called me, upset they weren't invited to the wedding."

"Take a look at your wife's left hand," Ron said. "I know a wedding ring when I see one."

Heat crept up Rachel's neck.

"Rachel was married before," Derek said smoothly. "She wears the rings to honor her deceased husband's memory."

"I never noticed 'em before," Ron said stubbornly.

Time to move on. Rachel flashed Ron a warm smile and changed the subject. "Where's your wife? I thought she was coming with you tonight."

"She's got that stomach bug that's been going around," Ron said. "Started yesterday. She's a little better today, but not up to a party."

"Be sure to tell her she was missed and that we hope she feels better soon," Derek said, slipping his arm around Rachel's waist.

His arm stayed there until all the guests had arrived. Then he took her hand and they started mingling.

Rachel slanted an admiring glance in his direction. "You're so good at this."

"At what?" he said, effortlessly scooping up a runaway cherry tomato from the floor and handing it to one of the waitstaff.

"At being a host."

"Well, you're an even better hostess."

"Are you kidding? I'm totally out of my element," Rachel said with a laugh. "I've never even had a dinner party at my home."

Derek's eyes widened in surprise. "You and your husband never entertained?"

"Tom wasn't much for socializing," Rachel said simply. "But despite my inexperience, I'm discovering that I like it. A lot."

He smiled and brushed a kiss across her lips.

At her startled look, he pointed to a spot directly above them where a sprig of mistletoe hung.

Rachel resisted the urge to touch her still-tingling lips. "Is it only my imagination or is there an overabundance of mistletoe in this house?"

"Travis's contribution to the party." Derek grinned. "He even put them up."

"It surprises me that he went to so much trouble. I mean, there aren't that many single women here," Rachel said.

"But the one woman he is interested in kissing is here," Derek said. "Mary Karen."

"Nah." Rachel shook her head. "He and Mary Karen are just old friends."

They'd just stepped into the kitchen when Derek grasped her arm and pulled her to a stop.

"Does that look like they're just friends?" Derek spoke in a low tone and gestured with his head to the doorway leading to the walk-in pantry.

Rachel inhaled sharply and widened her eyes. Travis and Mary Karen were kissing with a feverish intensity that brought heat rushing back to Rachel's cheeks.

When Travis's hand closed over Mary Karen's breast, Rachel had seen enough. She looped her arm through Derek's and pulled him to the other part of the large kitchen. Once there, she paused.

"She's had several glasses of champagne," Rachel

said, pulling her brows together in worry. "Do you think she knows what she's doing?"

"I think she knows exactly what she's doing and what she wants," Derek said with a chuckle. "And so does Trav. Those two have it bad for each other."

Rachel rolled her eyes. "I told you, they're old friends."

"Friends don't kiss each other like that," Derek pointed out.

"You kiss *me* like that," Rachel reminded him. "And you and I are just friends."

"About that." Derek cleared his throat. "I—"

"There you are." David rushed into the kitchen, his gaze focused on Derek. "I've been looking all over for you. It's time."

"For what?"

"For you to get into this suit and do your thing." David shoved a wadded-up bundle of red velour and white fur into Derek's hands. "Hurry, the kids are waiting."

"What is this?"

"What does it look like?" David chuckled. "It's a Santa suit."

"Why would I need one of those?"

"I must have forgotten to tell you." David's smile widened into a grin. "Whoever hosts the party plays Santa Claus."

By the time the last child had hopped off Derek's lap with their bag of goodies, his irritation at David's last-minute announcement had disappeared.

He'd planned on spending the entire evening with Rachel, not listening to squirming children recite their

"I wants." But he had to admit he'd enjoyed playing Santa. Not surprisingly, the experience had resurrected a long-forgotten memory of the times his father had played Santa Claus for the neighbor kids.

His father had been so patient, so kind. But what Derek remembered most was how, just before each child left his lap, he'd ask them what they wanted for Christmas that didn't cost money.

Derek remembered one year vividly. He hadn't yet realized that the man in the red suit was his father. He'd confided in Santa that he'd gladly give up all his gifts if his daddy could just be home more. That next year his father took a job where he didn't have to travel. Derek had never made the connection. Until now.

For fun, Derek had asked Mickie that same question. She hadn't hesitated. She'd told him she wanted Mr. Rossi and Rachel to get married and adopt her.

He'd promised to do his best, knowing it wasn't just Mickie's wish that would come true if that happened, but his as well.

Chapter Seventeen

"Anyone know how to play this?" July called out to the crowd, sliding her hand reverently across the top of the shiny black grand piano.

"I know how to play," Derek said when no one else volunteered. His mother had made both her children take lessons until they were well into their teens. Still dressed in the Santa suit, Derek made his way to the piano. "Is there something you'd like to hear?"

"'Santa Claus Is Coming to Town.'" July's gaze dropped to the nine-month-old on her hip. "It's one of his favorites."

"It's one of Santa's favorites, too." Derek gave a hearty ho-ho-ho and then pulled out the bench and sat down. He had to wedge his large stuffed belly between him and the keyboard. "But if I'm going to play, I'll need a couple helpers."

July shook her head when he glanced in her direction.

She gestured to the baby bouncing up and down in her arms.

Derek then turned to Rachel and Mickie who'd wandered close. "How about you two lovely ladies? Will you help out old St. Nick?"

When they hesitated, the guests in the area clapped and shouted encouragement.

"I don't know how to play the piano," Mickie said.

"But you can turn the pages of the sheet music, can't you?" he asked.

"As long as you tell me when to do it," Mickie said with an earnestness that touched his heart.

"It's a deal." Derek kept his voice deep and jolly. He then fixed his gaze on Rachel. "You look like a woman who knows her way around a piano."

Rachel lifted a hand, moving it side to side and took a step back. "I haven't played in years."

"Ho-ho-ho. No worries." Derek patted a spot on the bench beside him. "We'll play together."

Last week Derek had found a book of Christmas duets in the cabinet. Although he could easily play any Christmas song with his eyes shut, he found himself wanting to share the experience with Rachel.

"I don't know—"

"Surely you don't want to disappoint all these fine people?" He flashed his best Santa smile.

With obvious reluctance she sat beside him. Then, with the smile still on her lips, she leaned close to him and spoke between gritted teeth. "What part of 'I don't want to play' don't you understand?"

"Did everyone hear that? The lady wants old St. Nick to kiss her. Must be the mistletoe." Derek glanced up and she followed his gaze. He knew the exact moment she saw the tiny sprigs because her eyes widened.

He pressed a kiss against her lips. It was altogether unsatisfactory, thanks to beard interference.

"Blasted white fur," he muttered.

She chuckled.

Thirty minutes later, he and Rachel rose from the piano and bowed to riotous applause.

"Santa needs to get back to the North Pole," Derek told the children who begged him to stay. "The reindeer and elves are waiting."

With one last ho-ho-ho, Derek sprinted up the stairs. He reappeared minutes later dressed in the dark pants and gray shirt he'd worn earlier. After mingling for several minutes, he found Rachel by the window with her back to him.

He slipped his arms around her waist. "I was hoping you'd come up and help me change."

She turned in his arms, offering him a sexy smile. "I was tempted," she said, planting a kiss on his jaw. "But then I remembered that this is a G-rated event."

"Tell that to Mary Karen and Travis."

Rachel's gaze darted around the crowded room. "Where are they?"

"Last I saw, they were stumbling into the guest bedroom upstairs," he said.

"Oh, my." Rachel's mouth formed a perfect *O*. "What did you say?"

"I told 'em, don't do anything I wouldn't do."

Derek planned to say more, but she looked so beautiful and appealing in the firelight's glow that he pulled her to him and kissed her…under another sprig of mistletoe. He owed Travis a check for a job well done.

Despite being up late the night before, Rachel rose before the sun had come up and headed to the kitchen. She ground some beans and got the coffee brewing.

Three years ago to the day, Tom had gone out for orange juice and never returned. But surprisingly this morning her thoughts weren't on Tom but Derek. When she'd been with Tom, everything had revolved around their home life together. They hadn't socialized with friends or other couples because they hadn't needed anyone else. They'd had each other. It had been enough.

But as happy as she'd been, Rachel wasn't sure that a relationship of that nature would suit her now. She liked spending time with friends. She liked doing "couples" activities.

Rachel felt like a butterfly that had finally found its wings. The changes hadn't happened overnight, but rather had been occurring gradually these past three years. But Derek, well, he'd shown her how to soar.

"I love him," Rachel said aloud, the realization welling up from deep inside, the words right and strong against her tongue. "I love Derek Rossi."

She felt a momentary stab of guilt as her gaze was drawn to her wedding picture. Rachel crossed the room and picked up the frame. She slowly ran a finger across his lips, outlining Tom's smile. This man had been her friend. Her first lover. Her beloved husband.

She hugged the photo against her. Was that understanding she'd seen in her husband's eyes?

"Being with Derek in no way diminishes what I felt

for you," she whispered. "You taught me how to love and how to accept love. Even when it looked like we might never have a baby, you were so sweet, insisting that I was all you needed to be happy."

Tears welled in Rachel's eyes and spilled over. She let them fall, finding healing in them.

"Since you died, I've been just going through the motions of living." She sat the picture down and pulled the ring slowly from her finger. "I know that's not what you want for me. You want me to be happy. Derek can make me happy."

But can I make him happy?

Derek wanted children. Children she probably wouldn't be able to give him. It had been a struggle to get pregnant when she was in her mid-twenties. What would it be like now? She was a nurse. She knew the odds. *Practically impossible.*

Before there were any promises made, she would tell Derek about her infertility journey. She would hold nothing back. There would be no secrets between them. It would then be up to him. If he made the choice to walk away, she would try to understand.

Regardless of what he decided, it was time she moved on with her life. She placed her diamond in front of the picture. This way it would be the first thing Derek saw when he walked into the room.

Thinking back to those little boys and girls sitting on his knee, she found herself wishing she could whisper in his ear *her* one desire.

All she wanted for Christmas, all she would ever want in the future, was him.

* * *

Derek reached into his pocket making sure the tiny black velvet box was still there. Since he'd left Idaho Falls, he'd checked his pocket at least a half-dozen times.

Despite what his past engagement history would suggest, Rachel wasn't just another woman in a long line of women; she was The One. They shared the same values and enjoyed spending time together. Not just in bed, but out as well. As corny as it sounded, she was the half that made him feel whole. He couldn't wait to make her his wife.

Though the ring was burning a hole in his pocket, he told himself he wouldn't propose until after Christmas. When he popped the question he wanted it personal and private and perfect.

What if she says no?

The question came out of the blue and Derek immediately dismissed it. He was confident Rachel loved him. Although he'd initially worried he'd be competing with a dead man the rest of his life, Rachel's behavior said that wasn't an issue. She'd pursued him. She'd made it clear she wanted him. And her love was the only thing he wanted….

Not only for Christmas. But for eternity.

The Christmas Eve worship service at Jackson Hole Community featured the children of the congregation. While Mickie did a great job in the chorus, Addie's solo rendition of "What Child Is This" stole the show.

With Rachel seated beside him, Derek couldn't imagine being happier. While his feelings for her went far beyond the physical, he liked the way she looked tonight. The soft pink cashmere sweater with its bits of gold glimmer hugged her curves quite nicely. The matching skirt was long enough to be proper, but short enough to show off her gorgeous legs. And there was something about a woman in heels...

He leaned close, brushing a strand of hair back from her face. "Have I told you how incredible you look tonight?"

"Shh." Rachel gestured with her head toward the minister. But the flush in her cheeks told him that his compliment had pleased her, and when he reached over and took her hand, she curled her fingers around his.

After being ushered out to the large common area of the church, he and Rachel waited with Lexi and Nick for the children to be dismissed. The mood in the church was a festive one.

"Do you think we're supposed to go and get them?" Rachel asked Lexi when five minutes turned into ten.

Nick glanced at his watch. "If we're going to make the caroling, we need to leave pretty quick."

Every year, a local church invited citizens in the area to join them for caroling in the Jackson town square. With white lights on the arch made of antlers shining brightly and everyone holding candles, it was, according to Rachel, a not-to-be-missed experience.

"We'll go check." Lexi took Rachel's arm and the two women hurried off through the crowd.

"Hurry back," Derek said, watching until she disappeared from sight.

"I recognize that look," Nick said, an easy smile on his lips. "You've got it bad, my friend."

"I love Rachel," Derek said, overcome with the sudden urge to say it out loud and make it seem real. Waiting to propose until after Christmas was turning out to be a real challenge. "I plan to ask her to marry me."

"I'm happy for you, man." Nick slapped him on the back. "Mickie and Addie will be thrilled that all their efforts weren't in vain."

Derek pulled his brows together. "What are you talking about?"

"C'mon, you must have picked up on their matchmaking ploys." Nick shook his head and chuckled. "Though I have to admit a couple were fairly clever."

This was the first Derek had heard of this effort. He wondered if Mickie had said anything to Rachel. "How did you find out about it?"

"Addie told her mother." Nick shrugged. "Lexi told me."

Derek couldn't imagine what tricks an eight-year-old and a ten-year-old could employ. Still, he was curious. "What kinds of things did they do?"

Nick waved to Ron and his wife across the room before answering. "Simple things like making sure you and Rachel ran into each other to more complicated ones like using technology to their advantage."

Derek lifted a brow.

"There was something about a couple of text messages." Nick chuckled. "Apparently Mickie made it look like the texts had come from Rachel."

The knot in Derek's stomach twisted. If this were true it meant Rachel *hadn't* reached out to him after all. Had he built all his hopes on a false premise? On a lone text message she hadn't even sent?

"Interesting," he said, when he realized Nick was expecting a response.

"Harmless kids' stuff," Nick said. "But amusing. And quite ingenious."

"No denying those two are smart," Derek said, forcing a chuckle. He told himself this didn't change anything. Yes, he'd taken Rachel's text as a sign she was over Tom, he still knew—he *knew*—that Rachel loved him.

As much as Tom? a voice inside his head whispered. Derek clenched his jaw so tightly that his teeth ached. *She does love me,* he told himself. *If not more than Tom, at least as much.*

She had to…because he wasn't going to be second in a woman's life ever again.

Although there was no reason to get up early on Christmas morning, Mickie was awake by seven. She dressed quietly, not wanting to bother Rachel. But when she and Fred reached the kitchen, Rachel was already at the table.

"Good morning, Mickie." Rachel smiled a welcome.

"Merry Christmas." Mickie returned the greeting carefully. Rachel's eyes looked sad. Just like they'd been when she'd kissed Mickie goodnight.

Just thinking about last night made Mickie's stomach hurt. It had started out okay. Addie's mother had made a yummy dinner of chili and cinnamon rolls. And the church singing had gone well. It had been fun standing with the other kids and hearing everyone clap.

"Mr. Rossi kinda acted weird last night," Mickie said to Rachel.

"I think he was just tired." Rachel's words were reassuring, but the worried look in her eyes told a different story. "This has been a busy week for him."

"He was supposed to come over here after we sang in the square," Mickie reminded her. "We were going to decorate your tree together and then he was going to help me wrap your gift."

Instead, he'd made some lame excuse about needing to make a few phone calls. Maybe that was true, but it had reminded Mickie of the excuses Uncle Wayne used to give Aunt Amy.

"We'll see him this morning." Rachel smoothed a wayward strand of hair on the top of Mickie's head. "Why don't you let Fred out? He's been inside all night and it'll be good for him to…stretch his legs. But don't leave him out too long because it's really cold this morning."

Mickie headed to the back of the house, each step heavier than the last. She opened the door and let the air waft over her. Even after Fred ran past her, Mickie stood there a few moments longer. Rachel was crazy. It wasn't cold outside at all. When she finally shut the door, Mickie realized the reason Rachel thought it was so cold outside was because the house was so hot.

After wiping the sweat from her brow, Mickie went searching for a ribbon to put around Fred's neck.

Chapter Eighteen

Three hours later, Rachel and Mickie were still waiting for Derek to arrive. They hadn't settled on a definite time last night. Rachel had told him to come over some-time in the morning.

"When is he going to be here?" Mickie whined. "I thought you said we could open gifts at ten."

Keeping the child up last night had been a mistake. There were dark circles under her eyes. And all she'd done since she'd gotten up was complain. The child had never been this cranky, not even when they'd argued over Tom's pictures.

"Not long." Rachel finished covering the breakfast casserole with foil, then slid it back in the oven to keep warm. "You look tired."

Mickie shrugged.

"Fred looks tired, too. Why don't you take him to

your bedroom and lie down for a few minutes? I know he won't go without you."

"But the gifts—"

"I'll come get you the minute Der—er, Mr. Rossi, arrives."

To Rachel's amazement, Mickie didn't argue but padded back to her bedroom with the dog at her side.

Less than fifteen minutes later, a knock sounded at the front door.

"I'm sorry I'm late," Derek said, the second she opened the door. "I'd already made it to Jackson when I realized I'd forgotten the gifts and had to turn back."

Flakes of snow dusted his dark hair and she noticed he'd started wearing cowboy boots with his jeans, like most of the men in town.

Rachel stepped aside to let him enter, then quickly shut the door against the frigid north wind while he placed the presents under the tree and hung up his coat.

"I thought you'd be here earlier," she said when he looked her way.

"I wanted to be, but it took longer than I thought to finalize some...arrangements."

Rachel remembered Mickie's disappointed expression. "You could have called."

"I had so much on my mi—" He stopped himself. "You're right. I should have called. My apologies."

He glanced around the room. "Where's Mick?"

"She was Little Miss Whiny this morning," Rachel said with a sigh. "I suggested she rest a bit, but promised I'd let her know the second you arrived." Rachel turned toward the hall. "I better—"

"Wait." Derek reached out and touched her arm. "There's a part of your Christmas gift I wanted to give you privately. Let's take advantage of the opportunity."

"O-kay." Rachel's heart gave a little leap, then settled into an unsteady rhythm against her ribs. She sat on the sofa and he took a seat beside her. If he noticed her diamond ring next to Tom's picture, he didn't mention it. Maybe she should just tell him what was in her heart.

Nervous energy rolled off him in waves. He pressed an envelope into her hand. "This is the first part."

She opened the envelope with shaking hands. Two sheets of paper were nestled inside. Airline itineraries. One for her. One for Mickie.

"Tickets for us to L.A." Rachel lifted her gaze. "January 9 to 12."

"I'm receiving an award on the tenth for broadcast excellence," Derek said. "And I want both of you there with me."

Rachel heard the pride in his voice. Justifiable pride. The award was a sign, a very visible indication, that he'd successfully made the often-difficult transition from athlete to expert sports commentator.

"Congratulations." She wrapped her arms around his neck and gave him a big kiss. "You're a rock star."

He flushed with pleasure. "My mother and Jim, as well as my sister and her family are flying in." He took her hand. "It will be a great opportunity for you and Mickie to meet them. I thought we could—"

"I can't go." Regret made her voice thick.

His smile disappeared. "You can't? Why not?"

Please God, please. Help him understand.

"The community is dedicating a fallen heroes

memorial at the city park." Rachel spoke faster as storm clouds began forming in his eyes. "Most of the men and women being honored are fallen military and law enforcement, except for—"

"Tom."

He practically spat the name and her temper flared. Mickie wasn't the only one feeling the effects of a late night. But Rachel managed to keep a tight rein on her emotions, reminding herself that Derek was disappointed. But still, couldn't he see that she was disappointed, too? "If it were any other day, I'd love to—"

"Tom is dead. I'm alive," he continued as if she hadn't spoken. "You're telling me you'd rather stay here and commemorate the past rather than come with me and celebrate the future?"

"It's not just me, Derek. Tom's parents are flying in. The clerk he protected is coming. How can I not be there? I'm his wife and—" Rachel stopped. "I mean, I *was* his wife."

Derek jumped to his feet. "You got it right the first time."

Though he stood close enough to touch, she felt him slipping further and further away. A sudden desperation took hold. She rose to her feet. "Please, let me explain."

His expression gave nothing away. It was as if he was on the mound, bases loaded, no outs, the cool blue eyes saying he was in perfect control of the situation. But the tiny muscle jumping in his jaw told her he wasn't as composed as he appeared. He cocked his head. "The Friday night that I came over…when you were just getting out of the tub."

"What about it?"

"If I hadn't stopped by, would you have called and asked me over?" His penetrating gaze demanded nothing less than total honesty.

She wanted to say yes, but that would be a lie. Her emotions had been in turmoil then. She hadn't known what she wanted.

"Rachel?" he prompted.

"I don't know," she said after a long moment. "I'd like to say yes, but I really can't say for sure."

"Because of Tom. Because you knew you'd never love anyone like you loved him."

That *had* been what she'd thought at the time, but even then she'd felt a strong pull toward Derek. Most importantly, it wasn't how she felt now. "Yes, I thought that once, but—"

"That's all I needed to hear." He whirled and reached for his coat just as Mickie entered the room.

She was still in her flannel pajamas, her face flushed from sleep. "Merry Christmas, Mr. Rossi."

"Merry Christmas, sweetheart."

The girl's gaze settled on the coat in his hands. "Are you going somewhere?"

"I can't stay." He hesitated for a second and his eyes grew soft. "But I brought your presents."

Tears welled in Mickie's eyes and her shoulders drooped. But to Rachel's surprise the girl didn't argue. It was as if she'd seen this coming. Or maybe she'd just grown resigned to disappointment. "Can I at least give you a hug before you go?"

"Of course." Derek dropped his coat to the chair before crossing the few feet that separated them. He pulled the child into his arms and held her close for several heartbeats.

"I'll be in touch about you coming to Los Angeles," he whispered against her hair.

"Okay."

Derek's gaze narrowed. He pressed his palms against her cheeks. The furrow in his brow deepened. "Mickie, munchkin, you're hot. Too hot. How do you feel?"

"Sad." Mickie's face scrunched and she sniffed loudly.

"Derek, can't you at least stay until we open gifts?" Not only did Rachel hate to see Mickie disappointed, but she also desperately needed the time. Time to convince him that Tom was her past. Time to convince Derek that he was her future.

He shook his head and gave Fred a final pat on the neck.

Rachel fought the tears pushing against the back of her lids and turned her face. She couldn't watch him walk out that door knowing it might be the last time she'd see him. She simply couldn't. Instead she focused on Mickie and forced a bright tone. "Shall we eat or open gifts first?"

"I don't feel so good."

Rachel felt, rather than saw, Derek pause at the door.

For the first time since Mickie had entered the room, Rachel studied the child. Not with the eyes of a foster parent, but the eyes of a mother. Her cheeks were bright red while her skin was unusually pale. Fever dulled her normally bright eyes. Mickie wasn't tired, like Rachel had thought. She was *sick*.

What kind of nurse was she? Worse yet, what kind of mother didn't notice her child was ill?

Rachel crouched down. She placed her hand on the girl's forehead, then dropped it to her arm when Mickie began to sway. "Honey, you're burning up. We need to get you to bed. Can you walk? Or do you want to lie down out here?"

"I don't feel so good," Mickie repeated, her voice shaky.

"I'll carry her to the bedroom." Derek crossed the room in several long strides.

Rachel stepped to the side just in time for Mickie to throw up…all over Derek.

Derek hopped out of the shower, dried off, then tightened the belt to Rachel's fuzzy pink bathrobe around him.

After getting Mickie settled in bed, Rachel had confiscated his clothes and put them into the washing machine. He'd almost insisted on driving home to clean up, but the smell of vomit all over his shirt and jeans made him queasy.

He'd stood in the shower for a long time, washing the smell away and doing some hard thinking. Last night, after learning that Mickie had been the one reaching out to him, he'd found himself wanting to confront Rachel so he could get the reassurance he craved. The realization that it could end up ruining the evening for all of them had kept him silent. Still, he'd ended up cutting the night short when temptation threatened his resolve.

Now he had his answer. But it made no sense to be upset with Rachel. The fact that he'd fallen in love with her was *his* problem, not hers. She'd made it clear that she wasn't looking for a boyfriend. Or a husband.

Friends with benefits. He snorted. What a stupid label. And completely inaccurate. On his part anyway.

Of course she'd want to stay for her husband's memorial. Of course. Tom might be dead, but he was still the most important person in her life. Derek had been foolish to hope otherwise.

He glanced down at the fuzzy robe. When Rachel looked back on their time together, if she looked back, this would be how she'd picture him.

His lips twisted in a wry smile. Great. Just great.

But what was his choice. Hide out in the bedroom until his clothes were dry? Derek rejected that option immediately. He might be down but he wasn't out. And Mickie, he had to check on Mickie. He gave a tug on the belt to make sure it was secure and headed for the kitchen.

Rachel was standing by the counter when he strutted into the room looking like a peacock who'd overdosed on Pepto-Bismol.

He held up a hand when her lips twitched. "No jokes, please."

"But you look so pretty in pink." Even though she smiled, her eyes remained wary. Gracious to the end. Love for her rose up from the deepest recesses of his heart and spilled over. "How's Mickie?"

"She's been cleaned up, had a dose of Tylenol and is now asleep," Rachel said.

"What do you think is wrong? Stomach flu? Food poisoning? Has her fever dropped?"

"Stomach virus," Rachel said. "You don't get a fever

with food poisoning. And yes, thankfully, her temp is going down."

"She's lucky to have you." Derek wondered how he'd do, being both mother and father to Mickie. Better than a group home, he told himself. Better than someone like her aunt and uncle.

"It'll be another thirty minutes until your clothes are dry." Rachel gestured to the casserole she'd just pulled out of the oven. "I'm not sure if I should mention food after what you've just gone through but...would you like some breakfast? Or at least coffee?"

Though her words were conversational and pleasant, an underlying tension filled the room.

My fault, he reminded himself. *Not hers.*

"Actually I am hungry," he said.

A relieved smile was his reward. She dished up the food while he poured the coffee.

But once at the table, awkwardness settled over them like a shroud. They ate in silence. Finally Derek had had enough. He had some apologizing to do. And there was no reason to put it off any longer. He placed his napkin on the table and pushed his plate aside. "We need to talk."

"I agree." Her voice was calm, almost matter-of-fact. But when her napkin joined his on the table, he noticed her fingers were trembling.

Her very bare fingers. Where was Tom's ring?

Derek's heart rose to his throat. He pushed back his chair and stood. "I know you're probably upset with me after how I acted, but can we start with a hug?"

"I'll always take a hug from you."

When she came into his arms, he pretended not to

notice the tears in her eyes. She was warm and soft and the intoxicating scent of vanilla was oh so familiar. He pulled her close and his own eyes filled with moisture.

How can I let her go?

He tightened his hold around her.

"I wish we didn't have to sit down." She laid her head against his chest. "I wish we could stand here like this and talk."

"We're making the rules." Derek swallowed past the lump in his throat. "Nothing says we can't."

Nothing except he was finding it incredibly hard to keep his emotions under control. He felt raw, vulnerable. He had to apologize. Before he found his voice, Rachel began to talk.

"For seven years I loved Tom with my whole heart. Only Tom. I never thought that I could love anyone that much again." She cleared her throat. "Then I met you."

Derek's heart stopped for a second before resuming an unsteady rhythm.

"I convinced myself that you and I were just friends." Her voice grew stronger with each word. "But I can't lie to myself any longer. I love you, Derek."

Some of the tightness left his shoulders at the declaration. But how much? That was still the question….

"My love for you is different than my love for Tom had been, more mature. Deeper on so many levels." She hesitated, then met his gaze. "I truly believe you are my soul mate."

Derek had pitched a no-hitter against the Yankees. At the time he'd been convinced that nothing could top the high he'd experienced when that game ended. He'd been wrong. This moment defied all description.

She swallowed hard. "I'll go with you to Los Angeles."

"No," he said. "I was wrong to ask—"

"When I was getting Mickie in her pajamas, I saw one of the pictures I took the day we went skiing," she continued. "You and Mickie are my life now. My loyalty is to the living. Tom's parents can represent him at the ceremony."

But as much as he wanted her there with him, her generosity of spirit prompted Derek to dig deep into his own soul and find out just how much he loved Rachel.

"I can't let you do that." The rightness of his decision washed over him. "Your husband was a hero. You need to be there."

Her brows pulled together. "But I want to be with you at your ceremony."

"They'll be other awards," he said. "If it's okay, I'd like to be at your side when Tom is honored."

"You'd do that? You'd miss your own banquet?"

"I owe the man." He cupped her face gently with his hand. "Tom loved and cared for you all those years before I met you. He kept you safe and happy."

Rachel's eyes grew large. "Oh, Derek, I don't know what to say."

"That's not all." Derek had planned to wait but he couldn't hold back any longer. "I want to build a life with you, Rachel. Raise a family—"

She covered his mouth with her fingers. Her gaze searched his. He saw the hesitation, the fear. "Before you say anything else, you need to know that Tom and

I went through several years of infertility treatments before I finally got pregnant. They never discovered the problem, so it's a very real possibility that I'll never be able to conceive."

"And that's important…why?"

"Because you want a family and children of your own."

"No, I want children. That doesn't mean you have to give birth to them," Derek said. "We can adopt or take in foster kids. In fact, I called Mickie's social worker the other day and left a message. I told her I wanted to adopt Mickie."

"I left her the same message."

"You did? I thought you didn't think you could manage a child alone with your schedule?"

"I told myself love would find a way. I couldn't let her go, Derek. She's my daughter."

"She's my daughter, too."

Her gaze locked with his. In that moment, everything between them settled into something eternal.

"*Our* daughter. *Our* child." The joy in Rachel's eyes told him it was time.

"I have something to ask you." Reluctantly Derek stepped from her arms. "Wait here."

He went back into the living room in search of his coat. He stopped when he saw her wedding ring sitting on the ledge by Tom's picture.

Smiling, he rummaged through his pockets and returned several seconds later, a little box clutched in his fingers.

He'd never imagined proposing in a fuzzy pink bathrobe, but then from the second he'd gotten hit on the head by a curveball, nothing had gone as he'd planned. All the challenges, all the strange twists had brought him to this point with Rachel. Derek took her hand and dropped to one knee.

"You bring a joy, a completeness to my life that is beyond what I could ever imagine. I love you, Rachel. All I want for Christmas, all I'll ever want for the rest of my life, is you by my side." Derek flipped open the box and the large emerald-cut diamond sent rays of colored light scattering. "Will you do me the honor of becoming my wife?"

Tears slipped down her cheeks. For a second Derek felt a pang of fear. Then he saw the love shining in her eyes and the panic fled.

She held out her hand and he looked pointedly at her bare finger.

Her cheeks pinked. "I took Tom's ring off. It was time."

Any lingering remnants of doubt about his place in her heart disappeared forever.

"There are probably some memorable words I should say now, but the only one that comes to mind is *yes*." Her eyes glittered like sapphires in the light. "*Yes,* I love you. *Yes,* I'll marry you. And *yes,* I promise you'll never have to wear a pink robe ever again."

Derek laughed with relief and sheer joy. Then he slid the ring on her finger and they went together, arm in arm, to wake up Mickie.

Epilogue

Although it was only February, all signs pointed to spring at the Wildwoods Mountain Resort in Jackson Hole. Outside, the sky was clear blue and the sun shone brightly. Inside, red, yellow and white tulips, symbols of true and everlasting love, filled the great hall.

Rachel had envisioned her wedding as a small, intimate affair witnessed by close family and friends. But then her coworkers at the hospital had asked if they could come. And Derek's large extended family had made plans to attend. The ones who surprised her most were Tom's parents. At the ceremony honoring their son, they'd told her they'd be back to witness her walk down the aisle.

When they'd all gone out for dinner in January, Rachel discovered Tom's dad was a huge baseball fan. He and Derek had hit it off immediately.

The final addition to their guest list had been an even more pleasant one. At the last minute Lexi and Nick had decided to stay in Wyoming through the summer, allowing them to be part of the wedding party and sending Mickie over the moon with happiness.

Mickie followed as Addie twirled her way across the room. Addie was her very best friend in the world.

They'd been charged with keeping Fred out of trouble at the reception. When the bloodhound stopped by a table and sat down, Addie quit twirling and they decided to get some food.

Mickie glanced around the room, finally spotting her new parents by the stone fireplace. Her dad looked every bit as handsome as Ken in his black tuxedo, and her mom's wedding dress made her look like a fairy princess.

While Mickie watched, her dad began kissing her mom, which didn't surprise Mickie at all. He'd been doing that a lot lately. Lots more than Ken ever kissed Barbie. "We did it," Mickie said, expelling a happy sigh. "They're really and truly married."

"Puking was an excellent idea," Addie said in an admiring tone around a mouth filled with cake.

Mickie popped a butter mint shaped like a flower into her mouth. She saw no need to inform Addie that she'd been so sick on Christmas Day that she barely remembered what had happened. All she knew was that when she finally felt better, there was a new shiny ring on Rachel's finger.

"Did I tell you my mom is having a baby?" Addie

swiped off a big hunk of frosting from her cake with her finger, then put the plate with the cake next to Fred.

"No way." Mickie almost choked on her mint. "My mom is having one, too."

Mickie had been surprised but pleased when her parents had told her the news yesterday.

"Your baby will be friends with my baby," Addie said with a decisive nod. "Best friends. Just like you and me."

"My mom says we're going to build a house close to yours with room for lots of babies and some bigger kids like me," Mickie said. Like Addie's family, they'd live only part of the year in Jackson Hole. Mickie wasn't sure what California was like, but she didn't care where her home was as long as she was with her family. But she couldn't help being glad she'd still get to see Addie.

"Mickie."

At the sound of her name, Mickie looked up and saw her mom motioning for her.

"It's time for family pictures."

"Gotta go." Mickie jumped up and hurried across the room.

The photographer had just positioned them on the staircase when Fred galloped up, crumbs of cake around his mouth, remnants of the white gauzy bow Mickie had placed around his neck hanging askew. He surveyed the three of them, then plopped down in front of Mickie.

The photographer paused. "Do you want the dog in the picture?"

"Please. Please. Let him stay," Mickie urged.

"What do you think?" Derek asked Rachel.

She let her gaze run over him. He looked so handsome in his black tux that Rachel had difficulty keeping her hands to herself. She straightened his tie, then brought a finger to her lips. "Well, he *is* part of the family."

"Yippee," Mickie squealed.

Rachel glanced around the room, at the family and friends who'd come to help them celebrate their love, to the daughter who'd brought them together, then sideways at the man she loved more with each passing day. Contentment wrapped around her like a favorite coat. It seemed almost…sinful to be this happy.

While the photographer fiddled with his camera settings, Rachel leaned close to her husband's ear. "I've got a proposition for you. Want to round the bases with me tonight?"

Before he could answer, Mickie leaned back between them. "If you're playing baseball tonight, count me in."

Derek and Rachel exchanged a glance and burst out laughing.

Mickie gestured like she was pulling a steam engine's horn. "Woo-hoo. Baseball it is."

Rachel laughed so hard tears filled her eyes and slipped down her cheeks.

Mickie continued to pull the pretend steam engine horn adding a deep chug-a-chug sound.

Fred's sleepy eyes brightened and he began to bay.

The camera flashed.

"Got it," the photographer said.

Rachel wiped the tears from her eyes, trying to catch her breath. "That'll be one interesting picture."

"Not half as interesting as our life together is going to be." Derek slipped an arm around his wife and grinned. "Batter up?"

* * * * *

SPECIAL EDITION

HARLEQUIN®

A *Romance*

FOR EVERY MOOD™

Spotlight on

Classic

Quintessential, modern love stories
that are romance at its finest.

See the next page
to enjoy a sneak peek from
the Harlequin Presents® series.

"LET ME GET THIS STRAIGHT. Are you actually suggesting that I would stoop to that kind of game playing?"

Saul came out from behind his desk and walked toward her. Giselle could smell his hot male scent and it was making her dizzy, igniting a low, dull, pulsing ache that was taking over her whole body.

Giselle defended her suspicions. "You don't want me here."

"No," Saul agreed, "I don't."

And then he did what he had sworn he would not do, cursing himself beneath his breath as he reached for her, pulling her fiercely into his arms and kissing her with all the pent-up fury she had aroused in him from the moment he had first seen her.

Giselle certainly *wanted* to resist him. But the hand she raised to push him away developed a will of its own and was sliding along his bare arm beneath the sleeve of his shirt, and the body that should have been arching away from him was instead melting into him.

Beneath the pressure of his kiss he could feel and taste her gasp of undeniable response to him. He wanted to devour her, take her and drive them both until they were equally satiated—even whilst the anger within him that she should make him feel that way roared and burned its resentment of his need.

She was helpless, Giselle recognized, totally unable to withstand the storm lashing at her, able only to cling to the man who was the cause of it and pray that she would survive.

Somewhere else in the building a door banged. The sound exploded into the sensual tension that had enclosed them, driving them apart. Saul's chest was rising and falling as he fought for control; Giselle's whole body was trembling.

Without a word she turned and ran.

Find out what happens when Saul and Giselle succumb to their irresistible desire in

THE RELUCTANT SURRENDER

Available January 2011 from Harlequin Presents®

MARGARET WAY

Wealthy Australian, Secret Son

Rohan was Charlotte's shining white knight
until he disappeared—before she had
the chance to tell him she was pregnant.

But when Rohan returns years later as
a self-made millionaire, could the blond,
blue-eyed little boy and Charlotte's heart
keep him from leaving again?

Available January 2011

HRI7704

REQUEST YOUR FREE BOOKS!

2 FREE NOVELS PLUS 2 FREE GIFTS!

SPECIAL EDITION
Life, Love and Family!

SSE10R

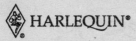

HARLEQUIN®

American ★ Romance®

C.C. COBURN
Colorado Cowboy

American Romance's
Men of the West

It had been fifteen years since Luke O'Malley,
divorced father of three, last saw his high school
sweetheart, Megan Montgomery. Luke is shocked to
discover they have a son, Cody, a rebellious teen on his
way to juvenile detention. The last thing either of them
expected was nuptials. Will these strangers rekindle
their love or is the past too far behind them?

**Available January
wherever books are sold.**

"LOVE, HOME & HAPPINESS"

www.eHarlequin.com

har75341